The Lullaby

Kirsten Miles

The Hummingbird Lullaby- Kirsten Miles

Copyright © 2024. All rights reserved.

ALL RIGHTS RESERVED: No part of this book may be reproduced, stored, or transmitted, in any form, without the express and prior permission in writing of The Elite Lizzard Publishing Company This book may not be circulated in any form of binding or cover other than that in which it is currently published.

This book is licensed for your personal enjoyment only. All rights are reserved. The Elite Lizzard Publishing Company does not grant you rights to resell or distribute this book without prior written consent of both The Elite Lizzard Publishing Company and the copyright owner of this book. This book must not be copied, transferred, sold, or distributed in any way.

Disclaimer: Neither The Elite Lizzard Publishing Company, nor our authors will manage repercussions to anyone who utilizes the subject of this book for illegal, immoral, or unethical use.

This is a work of fiction. The views expressed here do not necessarily reflect those of the publisher.

This book or part thereof may not be reproduced in any form, stored in a retrieval system, or transmitted in any form by any means-electronic, mechanical, photocopy, recording or otherwise-without prior written consent of the publisher, except as provided by Canada and USA copyright law.

In memory of my sweet grandmother, Gloria Aitken-Ross, who always encouraged my writing.

Chapter 1

I stare at my computer screen, willing myself to stay in my seat. This must have been the fifth time I have tried to edit this novel, and I'm becoming more frustrated by the second. In fact, working on this novel has been killing me. Feeling defeated, I change my browser and waste some time on Facebook. Maybe it will help me to relax.

As I'm scrolling along, I smile when I see Charli Diaz's status, which reads "This. Novel. Is. Driving. Me. Crazy." Laughing, I feel somewhat comforted by the fact that Charli's going through the same thing as I am.

Charli Diaz had been my favorite author as a child. She wrote amazing stories about fairies and princesses, but also of demons and dark lords- all the things I loved as a little girl. Years ago, she transferred over to writing for adults. Her latest novel, *It Takes a Village,* took the literary community by storm last year when it hit the best-seller lists on nearly every platform.

When I was just a little 20-year-old fangirl, I got to actually meet Charli and have lunch with her when she came to visit my college campus to make a speech. I still remember my eyes bulging in their sockets the first time I saw her.

She was even more beautiful in person than she is in that picture she puts on the back of all her books. Her bright blonde hair pooled across her shoulders like a golden fountain, and her even brighter eyes shined like rivers sparkling under the sun. She had such a genuine, warm expression that went beautifully with her perfect round face, highlighting her absolutely adorable dimples.

It was somewhat of an awkward experience, as I was almost too nervous to talk to her. I could barely look her in the eye and stuttered through different parts of the conversation. Yet, we ended up having a good chat. She was even kind enough to let me send her one of my manuscripts for feedback and was able to provide me with helpful writing tips. It was such a huge honor to have been helped by the well-known author.

For the past twelve years, Charli Diaz and I have kept in touch. Because she helped me with the novel I was writing, I had finally developed the courage to start my own publishing process. With time and effort- and Charli's extremely helpful pointers- I had become a published author by twenty-three, and my novel, *Fitting In*, had gained recognition in the literature world and won multiple awards.

Since that time, I admit I have not been writing very much. In fact, that book was published nine years ago now and I have wasted much of the decade drinking wine and watching *The Office* with my husband. It is almost as if I have been scared to write ever since I became a real published author. My book was so critically acclaimed that I became a big name in the industry for a while, but that eventually fizzled out. Although my book is still selling very well, and I am still a prominent name that is discussed in the literature communities, I have been too afraid to "pick up the pen" again. It is almost like I'm afraid that, if I write another book, it won't come close to my last one and my readers will be disappointed.

"I feel your pain," I write to Charli through Messenger. "How is your novel coming along?"

"Kate, it's so damn frustrating!" she responds. "I keep hitting the same wall over and over. I don't know what to do about these characters anymore."

"I'm always here to help!"

Ever since Charli helped me with my last project twelve years ago, she and I have been on friendly terms. Back then, she had given me helpful critiques, and we even met once for lunch to go over some basics before I started querying literary agents. I am no longer the scared, mousy little twenty-year-old who could hardly speak in front of her. Instead, I'm now thirty-two, an accountant, and a fairly confident young woman. Now, especially since I have become published myself, I no longer see Charli Diaz as this untouchable superhero whom I could never speak to like a normal person. Now, although we aren't exactly "friends," we mutually respect and support each other in our endeavors, and comment on each other's writing posts on Facebook sometimes.

Charli, of course, has published multiple books since I have last seen her. All of them have won awards for something. I have to admit, I'm a bit jealous when I think of it. Although my book was a success, I have been hungry for more acclaim and wanting to publish another. However, my writing is nothing like Charli's. While I have to struggle with syntax, Charli writes so effortlessly and easily, always making her books smooth and cohesive.

"I don't think anyone can help me with this," Charli responds, putting the emoji with the side eye next to it.

"I don't even know where to begin with my editing process," I write. "I think it's missing something. I don't know what it is, but it's definitely missing something." I put the emoji with a crooked smile beside it.

"I wanted to ask you," she writes, "if it isn't too much of a bother, if you would read my book. I understand if you're busy with your own, and you can say no. Ok?" I smile, feeling honored. Charli, much more well-known than I am, wants *me* to read *her* novel. My favorite author since I was just a little girl wants me to give her my professional opinion on her book. I am both honored and flattered.

"Of course," I write back. "I need a break from my own book for a while, anyway. Send it!"

I wait for her response as the little dots come across messenger. She then says, "Awesome.

Thanks so much. Can I have your email?" I give her my updated email address and then write,

"Actually, Mrs. Diaz, would you mind taking a look at my book, too? Only if you have the time. I can't imagine how incredibly busy you must be. I won't take any offense at all if you can't."

I wait for about a minute, chewing on my nails.

"Absolutely," she writes back. "I need a break from my book, too. Maybe we can get some inspiration from each other! And hey- call me Charli!"

I smile to myself. Despite feeling excited, I am nervous for her to read my book. What if she hates it? What if she doesn't like the way I write? What if it's not her style? What if it actually sucks?

She writes me her email address, and we agree to read each other's novels. I close my laptop and sigh. I am hoping that she'll be able to help me with mine. I am also really hoping her newest book has very little mistakes in it. Afterall, I have agreed to being a beta-reader. I absolutely cannot lie to her if the book has some critical mistakes in it. I would not be doing her a favor if I did that. At the same time, she is my favorite author and has been a mentor to me in the past, so the thought of critiquing her book is a bit daunting to me.

"Hey hon," says my husband, Richie, as he walks into my little makeshift home office. He leans over to kiss me.

"Oh, you're home early!" I say with a grin.

"I'm not sure if you sound happy or disappointed," he says with a laugh. I stand up and tell him about Charli and our agreement to read each other's novels.

"Wow," he says. "Sounds pretty exciting."

"Nerve-wracking," I say. "I'm not going to lie to her, so I hope I like it. I know she wouldn't lie to me either, so it's scary letting her read it."

"Well, all you can do is be honest," Richie says in that calm way of his. He is always so damn calm.

"Let's order something," I say as we walk down the hallway. "I'm starving."

After dinner, once I put the dishes in the dishwasher and feed our cat, Lila, I go back into my office and open up my laptop. I check my emails anxiously, but I haven't gotten anything from Charli yet. I open up a new email and attach my own story, sending it with a "Thanks so much! Take your time!"

I'm happy at the thought of reading another one of her novels- this time, me being the first one.

Afterall, my job at the bank could be so boring that it is grueling, and this would give me something new to focus on.

I cringe when I think of her reading my own book. It is nothing like my last- which was based more for kids- and this book has a lot of adult themes. In fact, it's a very sexual book, and I have been experimenting more with writing about sex. Not only do I find it interesting, of course, but I also know readers will too, which is why the sex in the book seems important. But the thought of my good ol' mentor reading it is a bit- well, awkward.

I sigh and cross my fingers. I am hoping with every cell in my body that Charli is impressed by my book. I am not sure what I will do if she hates it, and it makes me anxious to think that she may very well think it's bad. What if I think *her* book is bad? I highly doubt it.

As I change browsers to go on Facebook, I hear the little mail sound. When I click on it, it is Charli. She has sent me her story.

"*The Hummingbird*," it is called. Such a simple but beautiful title.

I save it on my computer and put it away. Afterall, it is getting late, and I have to get ready for work the next day. I tell myself that I will start reading it tomorrow, when I have some time and am sitting at my computer doing nothing.

Surely enough, I get that lull in the day to start reading Charli's book at work. I am initially very reluctant to start reading it. I pride myself on being an honest person now, not a scared little mouse, and I know I will tell her the truth. Of course, I'll be nice either way, but I will not lie to her. Afterall, she is depending on me to give her honest feedback and I would not be doing her due diligence if I were to just tell her everything is perfect.

I bring up the Word Document on my computer, looking around me to make sure my boss is nowhere to be found (which he rarely is anyway). It gives my heart a little thud when I see her name under her title. To think that I, Kate Benson, am about to proof-read my favorite author's novel is beyond my wildest dreams.

I take a deep breath and begin reading the first chapter. I am hooked immediately.

'The Hummingbird By Charli Diaz'

When Violet spread her towel on the sand at the beach, she was almost ready to just pack up and go home. It had taken her forever to find parking and even longer to walk down the street and over to the sand. But, because she had promised herself this would be the day, Violet stayed.

There were plenty of ways that Violet could end her life. However, she had always had a fondness for the beach, and she thought that this would be a good way to go out.

She brought nothing with her except her towel, her wallet, and the "exit bag"- the contraption she was going to use to fall asleep forever in the sand. She didn't even bring her phone, knowing that if she received a text or a call from anyone, she may not go through with her plan. It had taken her months to get up the courage to do this, and any little thing could deter her.

Violet couldn't have any more deterrents. She knew for a fact that her depression was not getting any better, despite how many electroconvulsive shocks or medication she was given, and her life had become what she considered a burden for her and the people around her. She had no reason to continue with a life that seemed to always want to destroy her.

Taking a look out onto the horizon, Violet sighed. This would be her very last day on earth and this would be the last view. It was a good view, too, with the waves crashing in front of her and the little seagulls dipping their heads into the water. She knew this was a really nice way to end everything.

After some time watching the waves, she began to cry, knowing that what she was about to do would make many people sad. However, in her mind, she believed herself to be better off dead- for both herself and for everyone else. Not only did she not see a point to living, but she truly thought that her family and the few friends she had left were sick of her depression and constant hospitalizations.

No, she thought stubbornly. *I won't do this to them. This is it.*

She took out the exit bag, preparing to set up. She knew that all she needed to do was put her head into the bag and fall asleep. Then, luckily, she would never wake up again.

Violet's hands were shaking. She knew that this would be the hard part- once the bag was in the right position. This was the part where she had to have the biggest guts she had ever had in her life. There was nothing else to do now but lay down.

Taking a deep breath and wiping a tear away from her face, she nodded to herself resolutely. She knew that this would be the right thing for everyone.

Just as she laid down and was about to put the bag around her head, something caught her eye. Well, not something, more than some*one*.

Violet sat up quickly. No one could see what she was doing, otherwise they would rescue her and ruin the plan. She threw the bag under the towel quickly, cursed God for once again making her live another moment, and looked to her side.

A few yards away was a captivatingly beautiful young woman. She looked to be younger than Violet- thirty or so- and was sashaying into the water like she didn't have a care in the world. She wore a beautiful salmon-colored sundress with a trendy white overcoat, her shoes little wedges that were the color of the sand as her feet splashed the ocean. Her hair was long and a beautiful auburn-brown and was catching the wind as she spun herself around. She was just close enough for Violet to see that she was smiling.

As Violet stared at her in trance-like bewilderment, the woman stopped running into the water and looked over at her. Violet quickly looked down at the sand, hoping that she didn't look like she had been staring at her.

To both Violet's surprise and horror, the woman began walking towards her direction.

Violet said a silent prayer that the woman would walk past her, like any other normal person would, but instead the woman approached her blanket and said in a friendly voice, "Hey! What time is it?"

When Violet looked into her eyes, she was transfixed by their beauty- the brown rims, the blueish-green around the pupil. She found herself unable to look away. Then, shaking herself out of it, she said, "I'm sorry, but I actually don't have my phone with me."

She knew this sounded strange. Who *didn't* have their phone with them at all times?

The young woman looked momentarily disappointed before saying, "Ah, well, that's ok. I was supposed to go to this party later but, honestly, I'm dreading it anyway. This must be a sign not to go then." Violet tried to smile but only nodded.

"I'm sorry if I'm bothering you," the young woman said, "and I promise I'll leave you alone, but do you know of any cool bars around here?"

Violet, unable to look directly into those stunning eyes, nodded. "There's a pretty good one about ten minutes down the road that way. It's called 'Sea Gert's.' They have great seafood there, too."

"Oh, I don't care about the seafood," said the beauty. "I just want to drink! You know those days where everything seems to be going wrong and you just need to escape?"

Did she? Yes. In fact, that was just about *all* Violet knew at this point.

"I do," Violet answered, this time forcing herself to smile despite the anger that her plans to die were being thwarted.

The woman smiled, showing teeth perfect enough to be in a dental magazine.

"I'm not from around here," she explained. "I guess you knew that, though. I'm from Pennsylvania, but I'm here for the summer. I'm staying with my cousin, Danny. He lives a few minutes from here. It's a far walk, though, but I don't mind because I like to walk. Any time I can be out in the sun, you know?"

Violet didn't know what to say except to nod.

"I'm sorry I'm talking your ear off," the woman giggled. "It's just that I haven't talked to another girl in two weeks! I guess I've been a bit lonely."

"I'm sorry to hear that," Violet answered.

The young woman gave her a curious look and said, "I'm Melanie. Do you live far?"

Violet shook her head. "It takes me about ten minutes to drive here. I'm Violet. It's nice to meet you."

Melanie's gorgeous tropical eyes lit up. "I'm not sure how busy you are, but I'll probably check out Sea Gert's a bit later. Do you feel like coming with?"

Violet's whole body froze. She absolutely did *not* feel like "coming with." This was not exactly her plan for the night. Violet always got a bit tongue-tied around other people so, in an attempt to be polite, she said, "Um…sure. I'm not doing anything tonight. I'll go with you. If you're alright with that."

Melanie's face lit up. "I'm more than alright with that! I'm so sick of my cousin and all of his disgusting friends. All they do is hit on me all the time. I'd rather be in the company of a woman any day!"

The last statement made Violet blush.

"I'm not in the best outfit for it," said Violet, referring to her baggy swim trunks and tattered button-down cotton shirt.

"Do you think I'm going like *this*?" said Melanie with a laugh, demonstrating her point by waving her arms across her body.

Violet didn't understand what she meant, as Melanie looked gorgeous.

"I need to get out of these shoes anyway," Melanie continued. "They're cute, but not kind to my feet. I think it's only, like, 6pm now. How about we meet…hmm. Let me think. How about we meet at Sea Gert's at 8:30 tonight? That'll give both of us enough time to go home and then get ready."

Violet nodded, in complete disbelief that any of this was happening.

"Ok," she said. "8:30 then."

"8:30!" confirmed Melanie excitedly. "I better start walking home now! It'll take me a while."

"I would drive you, but my entire car is completely full of crap," Violet said, allowing herself to give a small laugh.

"Don't worry, I'm used to the walk," assured Melanie. "I'll be ok. I'll see you there, 8:30!"

"I'll be there!" said Violet, watching Melanie as she turned, waved, and walked happily away. Her gait was free and lively, and she seemed to float effortlessly in the air, like she was dancing on clouds. It was hard not to stare at her.

She waited a moment before wrapping the exit bag with her towel and heading back to her car. How could she possibly commit suicide now? This woman had interrupted her peace completely, and Violet wanted her mind to be almost clear of anything at this point.

Getting back into her car, Violet sighed. She had no plans of returning home that day- or ever, in fact. Yet, there she was, driving back to her sad, little house.

I stop reading when I get a call from a customer, and it turns out that I am busy the rest of the day.

Wanting nothing more than to read Charli's novel, I am pretty pissed that I actually have to do my job. It is dull enough as it is, and I am becoming soaked into Violet's story very quickly. I long to see how her meeting with the young woman goes at the bar and if the two of them eventually become friends.

My day doesn't get easier as, racing home to read more, I get pulled over by the police and earn myself a speeding ticket. I am fuming mad by the time I get home. As soon as I walk through the door, my cat Lila pukes all over the floor, and I am forced to clean that up. Right after that, Richie gets home and talks my ear off about his job and how the customers at the hotel are horrible. I pretend to be interested but, to be honest, I just want to read Charli's book.

However, I don't get to that day. By the time Richie stops yammering on about work, it is time for dinner and time for me to cook. After dinner, Richie insists we watch a movie and, although it is ok, I am frustrated. It's hard to pay attention to something so mundane when a world of Charli's creation is just a couple rooms away.

After the movie, I am too exhausted to read, and I want to give Charli's novel my absolute full attention. I end up falling asleep, my plans to read her novel squelched.

Chapter 2

I can't believe how busy work is the next day. The one time I actually have something to do there, I can't do it. But, this time, I am determined to read Charli's book no matter what it cost me later on.

Before I leave work, I get a ping on my phone. It is an email from Charli and my heart jumps.

Charli: "I got your book. This week is crazy, so it might take a bit of time, but I can't wait to read this!!"

I smile to myself and tell her to take her time. I *want* her to take her time and savor every word of it. I am praying to God that she doesn't think it's terrible. I know my book needs a *lot* of work, but I hope she can at least see some good in it, too.

When I get home from work, Richie texts me saying that he is stopping over his mother's house to help her with her television. I laugh, as Richie couldn't fix a TV if anyone paid him a million dollars. Either way, I admire that he's trying.

This gives me a perfect window of a couple of hours to get soaked back in to Charli's novel. I take my laptop and sit on the couch, feet curled under me and a cup of ginger tea on the table. Lila comes to sit next to me, and I finally feel at peace. I bring up the novel on my computer and begin reading Violet's tale again.

Violet arrived at Sea Gert's bar at 8:30 promptly. That was something Violet was very good at- being prompt.

Looking around, there was no sign of Melanie. She decided to sit at a table on the side where she could watch the door. She was nervous and couldn't help but play with the ring on her finger. The same ring her grandfather had given her before he passed away. The same ring she hoped to be buried with.

It was about twenty minutes later, and Violet was nearly convinced Melanie would not show, when she finally did. Swinging open the door and bringing enough vitality in to drown the place with life, Melanie walked in, found Violet, and sat down, throwing her hand bag to her side.

"Well, this is cute! So beachy!" she said with a big smile, showing her unnaturally perfect teeth. "I can see why you like it here."

Violet smiled and nodded but could not speak. Getting a better look at Melanie was like staring into the sun- she was almost too beautiful and full of light that it might be dangerous. Her long, silky, brown hair flowed around her shoulders and down her tanned, perky breasts, and her brown-green-blue eyes held a look of both mystery and openness. Her nose was perfectly aligned to her face, her eyelashes bold and long, and her smile was sincere, the little folds on the side being the only thing that made her look older than twenty. She was very youthful, and Violet wondered if she was even in her thirties yet.

Just then, a waiter came over and took their orders. Melanie ordered herself two beers and a plate of cheese fries. Violet ordered the lobster and a beer for herself.

"Nice atmosphere," Melanie commented, looking around. Then, she stopped to smile at Violet.

Violet's head began to spin, and she hadn't even had a sip of beer yet. This *must* be because Violet was jealous of her looks. Melanie was so beautiful that she could be in a catalogue. That must be why Violet felt so drawn to her- it was jealousy.

"I like it here," said Violet. Suddenly remembering that she had a social duty to be polite, she forced herself to smile. "I used to come here with my friends- well, when I had friends."

Melanie looked surprised. "What happened to your friends?"

Violet sighed, not wanting to explain that her friends had abandoned her once her depression worsened about two years ago. Well, most of them did. The other two, Violet had pushed away herself.

"We all got kind of busy," explained Violet. "Once you turn thirty, people kind of separate a bit."

Melanie nodded. "That's scary. I'll be thirty in only two months!"

Violet smiled knowingly. She sat up a bit straighter in her seat and was careful not to smile so wide that her gums showed. Afterall, that wouldn't be very attractive. And Violet wanted to be attractive only due to the jealousy she had of Melanie's beauty. That was the *only* reason, she told herself.

The waiter brought the beer and food, and Melanie began to dig in like she hadn't eaten in days. Violet was a bit too shy for this approach, although she had to admit that she was hungry. Instead, she took a few large gulps of beer, praying that it would help her to feel less shy around Melanie.

"You drank that down!" Melanie laughed when Violet finished her beer in only a few minutes. "Here, have my second one for now. I'll order another one when I finish mine."

Reluctantly, Violet agreed, but sipped this one instead lest she have too much to drive home.

"Thanks for meeting with me here," said Melanie in her upbeat, excited voice. "I love my cousin and all, but I was *so* sick of spending all my time with his lame friends."

Violet liked the way she talked. So full of energy.

"You said you're from Pennsylvania," said Violet. "It must be nice to see your cousin."

Melanie sighed. "Well, I hadn't seen Danny in a long time. We were so close as kids, but we drifted apart in our teen years. Danny invited me to this beach house and I thought, what the hell? Why not? It's been, like, a thousand years since I've been to the Jersey shore!"

Violet nodded. "It does have its perks; I will say that."

Melanie took a swig of her beer. "Can I ask how old you are? I mean, you're obviously younger than I am, but I'm curious."

This made Violet laugh so hard she nearly spit out her beer.

"What?" asked Melanie with concern.

Violet composed herself. "I am *not* younger than you. I just turned thirty-five."

Melanie's mouth dropped. "Wow! You have great skin! How do you do it?"

"It seems like you don't need my help with that," said Violet softly.

Melanie shrugged her shoulders and gave Violet a very endearing smile. That feeling of her heart in her throat came over Violet again, and she, once again, shook it off as jealousy.

"I'm glad I met you," said Melanie sincerely. "Not just because I was sick of the guys."

Violet's heart had not come down from her throat yet, and this statement solidified that.

"I'm...glad I met you, too," said Violet.

Melanie's whole face lit up at that.

"Well, what do you do for work?" she asked.

"I'm an art teacher," answered Violet. "I teach college kids mainly, but sometimes the library hires me."

"Art!" exclaimed Melanie. "I *love* art! I can't draw a circle to save my life, but I do love to look at art."

"It's rewarding at times," answered Violet.

"How long have you loved art?"

Violet considered. "I guess my whole life. I don't remember a time when I didn't love it."

Melanie stared deeply into her eyes as if soaking up every single word. "I love going to museums. My friends say I'm crazy, but I don't give a shit what they say."

Violet giggled, brushing a piece of her black hair out of her face. She found herself desperately wanting to impress Melanie for some reason. Maybe it was to compete with her? Violet knew that she had always despised competition, so it couldn't be that. Maybe it was the jealousy just getting to her.

"I recently went through a break-up," said Melanie after a few moments of silence. It was the first time Violet saw her look sad, and it was a scene that Violet hated to see.

"Oh?" asked Violet. "Break-ups are terrible. If you don't mind me asking, what happened?"

Melanie sighed and looked out the window. Taking another sip of beer, she said, "Me and my ex had this huge fight. It started out as something stupid- like who was to pay for the movies- and then it just turned ugly out of nowhere. We started fighting about money all the time, and my ex kept insisting that I was over-spending when I was just spending my own money on shit I liked."

Violet took a sip of beer. "Men," she said, shaking her head.

She was surprised when Melanie giggled. "Oh, no," she said. "I haven't dated a guy since I was a freshman in college! This was an ex-*girlfriend*."

Violet nearly spit out the beer she had been sipping daintily. She had not expected that.

"You look shocked," said Melanie, still smiling. "I hope you're ok with the fact that I'm a lesbian."

Her pronouncing this just made Violet more surprised.

Attempting to look natural, she said, "Of course, I'm ok with it."

Melanie giggled again and asked the waiter for another beer.

"Are you going to be ok to drive home?" asked Violet.

"Oh, I knew I was going to drink so I'm taking a Lyft."

Violet, feeling a bit grateful that she had been rudely thwarted from her earlier plans that day, felt her heart softening.

"I'll give you a ride," she said. "My car is a filthy mess, just filled with art supplies. As long as you're ok with that, let me take you home."

Melanie's face lit up at this offer. "I don't give a shit how messy your car is. I'd be happy for you to take me home."

Violet couldn't help but smile. For a few minutes, she had almost forgotten about her sinister plans. For a few minutes, she almost felt like her old self- her cheerful, extroverted, *normal* self.

The girls talked a bit more about their lives and Violet found out that Melanie's father had died when she was very young. Her mother was addicted to drugs and wasn't around for much of Melanie's life, so Melanie ended up fending for herself most of the time. She even pushed her way through college on scholarships.

This would be a *lot* of information for just meeting someone for the first time, yet Violet didn't mind. In fact, she kind of liked Melanie's honest and frank way of talking. Violet herself did not give too much of her own life away, as she was more of a reserved person, but she let Melanie talk.

"You're a bit of a mystery, aren't you?" asked Melanie, looking into her eyes so deeply that Violet was nearly totally transfixed.

Violet shrugged. "Not really. I guess there isn't very much to say about me."

Melanie gave her a side smile. "I have a feeling that isn't true."

In a few moments, the girls got up and left the money on the table. After getting into Violet's car, Melanie- without even asking- hooked her Spotify up to Violet's car and began playing *Shape of You* by Ed Sheeran. Normally, this would have annoyed Violet but, for some reason, it didn't this time. This little bold action perfectly correlated with Melanie's outgoing and free-spirited personality.

"What's your favorite kind of music?" asked Melanie as she stuck her arm out of the car window and pretended to make waves with her hand.

"I'm not sure," said Violet. "To be honest, I like 80's rock and pop."

Melanie laughed. "The 80's! That's totally cool! I wish I had been alive back then."

Violet, barely alive herself in the 80's, giggled. She was not used to giggling like that since she was in her twenties, and it surprised her.

"I like that one song, 'Africa,' by Toto!" Melanie declared. "I think that was the 80s?"

"Yes," answered Violet. "What's *your* favorite music?"

Melanie paused as if she was about to share a secret. "It's really weird. I don't think I want to tell you."

Now, Violet *had* to know. Melanie had, at this point, practically confessed her whole life story to her, so what could possibly make her not want to tell her something so simple like her favorite music?

"I won't judge you," Violet assured her. "I listen to some strange music sometimes, too."

Melanie sighed. "I like almost any song about sex. It doesn't even matter the genre. It's normally RnB, but it can also be electronic, rap, hip-hop, pop- most of the main genres. But usually there is a theme of sexual passion in nearly all of my music."

This didn't exactly surprise Violet but, at the same time, she was somewhat surprised that Melanie was this forthcoming. Afterall, she didn't even *know* her.

"Ok," said Violet, not sure what else to say. "That's not so strange."

Melanie laughed, changing the song to *Shades of Cool* by Lana Del Rey.

"I love Lana Del Rey," Violet couldn't help but comment. "She's one of my favorite singers."

"No way!" cried Melanie. "Me too! *Music to Watch Boys To*? Sexy as hell. *Say Yes to Heaven*? So passionate!"

Violet giggled uncharacteristically again. "*Black Beauty* is a good one, too. Oh, I like all of her songs."

"Me, too, Violet."

Violet's chest tensed up when she said her name. It was the first time Melanie had said her name, and it was like music to her ears, the way she said it.

It was all too brief when Violet dropped Melanie off at her cousin's house.

"Thanks for the ride," said Melanie with that confident ease she had about her. "Wait- Violet?"

"Yeah?"

"Let's do this again. Tomorrow I've got to watch my nephew- well, he's my cousin's kid but I see him as a nephew- and then we're all going out to dinner. What about Monday night? If you're not too tired?"

Monday night. Earlier that day, Violet never thought she'd see a Monday night again. But now, it seemed as though it may not be so bad. Not this week, at least.

Violet smiled. "I think I'll be fine. Let's do it."

Melanie's pretty face lit up again and she got out her phone. They exchanged numbers and when Violet drove back to her lonely little house, she was almost glad to be there. *Almost*.

I am immediately mesmerized by the book. Charli is a published author, so her book would obviously be good, but *this* is nothing short of mesmerizing. I find myself already relating to Violet- a bit reserved, sometimes a bit shy even, and also not completely comfortable with who she is. Even her depression is relatable to me, and I am so anxious to see what happens to Violet.

I find myself a bit shocked and uncomfortable to read about Melanie being a lesbian. I am absolutely not homophobic in the slightest bit, so I'm not entirely sure why it's making me feel uneasy. I think I am more surprised because it isn't something I expected Charli to write. Her children's books were, well, obviously for children, and her last adult novel had only strictly heterosexual characters. This time, Charli is showing a different side of her writing abilities. She's also showing a different type of character than she has before. And she's doing a *really* good job at it.

I continue to read on and on that night. Even when Richie comes home, in a bad mood due to not being able to fix his mother's TV, I am reading. I just *have* to see if Violet ends up living or killing herself in the end.

I read along as Violet and Melanie go out to Sea Gert's again and learn more about each other. Violet remains timid and reserved, while Melanie brings the life everywhere she goes. They go out again, this time to the beach during the day, and Melanie tells Violet that she's always been attracted to girls for as long as she remembers. Kind of like me, Violet is uncomfortable to hear that. Violet is so much like me.

As I continue reading, Violet decides not to kill herself just yet, but is still planning on doing it at some point. But first, she wants to get Melanie through the summer. She doesn't want her new friend to mourn for her when being already so alone there. So, Violet makes a pact with herself to live until the end of the summer.

The book is beautiful, and I want to savor every single word of it. I am beginning to grow tired so I close my laptop, change into a nightgown, and finally let Richie bitch to me about his mother and her television. I can't help but only half-pay attention. I am too busy consumed in Violet's story and if her friendship with Melanie will end up saving her life.

Chapter 3

"Call Melanie," Violet said into her phone as she drove to get her hair done.

It had been approximately four years since Violet had anything done to her hair by an actual salon. Violet hadn't cared about her looks for years, not since the depression worsened. But now, strangely enough, Violet wanted to look pretty- because she was going out more. At least that's what she told herself.

"Hey girl hey!" yelled Melanie into the phone. "So where do you want to go tonight?"

Violet couldn't help but smile at Melanie's wild enthusiasm. "Did you want to check out that weird bar we saw when we were driving the other day? The one with the big shark on the roof?"

She could hear Melanie giggle on the other end.

"Actually, I had another idea," she said mysteriously.

This was one of the things Violet found so charming about Melanie. She was so honest about her feelings, but she also kept some of her eccentric ideas in her head.

"What's that?"

A pause. "I always wanted to sit and drink wine on the beach. I know that sounds silly, but I don't get to do that often in Pennsylvania. I say we sneak onto the beach tonight and pour ourselves a glass of wine! Maybe tell secrets and listen to Lana Del Rey?"

Only Melanie would say something like that in such a serious tone.

"I guess we can do that," agreed Violet. "Yes, let's do it. Why the hell not?"

"Why the hell not!" Melanie repeated with a laugh. "Ok, so did you want to meet at the same place we met before? The part of the shore right near that spa on Finn Street?"

"Ok!" said Violet, perhaps too enthusiastically. "Sure. Let's go around 9pm?"

"Sounds perfect," answered Melanie. "Ciao bella!" and she hung up.

Violet's hands started to shake on the steering wheel, she was so excited. It must have been the idea of drinking wine on the beach that made her feel suddenly so enthusiastic.

Upon arriving at the beach that night, it was Melanie that had gotten there first. She had spread out an enormous fuzzy hot-pink blanket and was, herself, wearing a hot-pink belly shirt with very short black shorts that were more like opaque tights.

That feeling hit Violet again. She had already admitted to herself that it was not jealousy, but very simple admiration for Melanie. She just *admired* her, like any other friend. She merely enjoyed her company and that was why she was so glad to see her.

"You look beautiful," Melanie commented, looking at her up and down.

This made Violet blush feverishly.

"I look like a mess," Violet answered with a short laugh, looking down at her very simple blue plaid sundress and plain wood sandals.

Melanie shook her head and then sat down on the blanket, patting the spot next to her. Violet did as she was told, perfectly obedient. It was as if Melanie had some sort of psychic power over her, some way of making Violet want to listen to her every demand.

For a few minutes, both girls said nothing. Instead, they continued to stare out at the beach, the stars poking through the dark sky and the moon making the waves look majestic. When Violet glanced over at her friend, she noticed that she looked very sad. It was a look Violet hadn't seen on her before.

"What's wrong, Melanie?"

Instead of smiling as usual, Melanie continued to stare out at the ocean. Then, very softly, she said, "Have you ever wanted something you couldn't have?"

"Yes," said Violet, thinking of the time she fell in love with her boss at the restaurant she worked at. "It's awful. What are you thinking about?"

Melanie shrugged and said simply, "I wish people were less judgmental."

"Yes," Violet agreed carefully. "Me too."

They were silent for some more time. Then, remembering the wine, Violet took a bottle of pinot grigio out from her beach bag and held it playfully in front of Melanie's face.

"Playful" wasn't a typical word to describe Violet, and it also surprised herself. Yet, she found herself in more and more of a playful mood around Melanie.

Melanie, seeming to feel the emotions, looked at Violet and smiled, the sadness finally defeated.

"You read my mind," she said as she took out her bottle opener. Hearing the spritzy sound, Violet reached into her beach bag and presented two plastic wine cups.

"As much as I wanted to be fancy, the glass ones would have definitely broken on the way over here," Violet said, laughing in a care-free way that she hadn't in a very long time. "Let me pour it."

Melanie held out her cup and Violet poured the dazzling liquid inside. Melanie still looked a bit downtrodden, and Violet wanted to do nothing but hug her friend suddenly.

They sipped their wine, Melanie chugging hers, and soon they were on their second glass. Violet was feeling nice and relaxed now, perhaps too relaxed. Melanie laid down onto the blanket and began to laugh, her whole body shaking.

"What's so funny?" asked Violet, herself laughing just from Melanie's contagious way about her.

Melanie continued to giggle for a while before looking over at Violet. Then, with so much conviction in her voice, she said, "I never expected to make a new friend here. I was just being silly and dancing on the fucking beach, and then I look over and see you in the sand. I have to be honest. I already knew what time it was. I just asked you because I wanted to talk to you."

Violet was shocked. "Why?"

Melanie half-sat up and looked out at the water. "I guess I could just feel your energy from all the way over there. I know that makes, like, zero sense."

"It does," Violet said quickly. "It does make sense."

When Melanie looked over at her, Violet's heart stopped. She wasn't sure if she had just reached an epiphany or if it was the wine, but, in that moment, Violet stopped bullshitting herself. When looking into Melanie's eager, youthful eyes again, she realized that it was more than just mere admiration for a good friend. She was falling in love with her. As scary as it was, she knew that she was falling in love with Melanie.

Melanie looked away from Violet for a moment. Suddenly, she said, "Have you ever kissed a girl before? I know you're straight, but have you ever kissed a woman?"

Violet began to laugh at the one awful memory she had of kissing a girl. "Well, yeah. One time in college. But everyone was drunk, and we were all playing spin-the-bottle. It was awful because the girl was so drunk she passed out as soon as we kissed."

Melanie began laughing again. "Oh no! That's so terrible!"

Violet looked over at Melanie. "Other than that, no, I've never kissed a girl."

Melanie opened her mouth to say something but stopped herself and looked out across the ocean sadly instead.

Violet took another gulp of wine. She was feeling a bit dizzy and maybe a bit tipsy, and it made her feel brave. Without looking at her, she reached over and placed her hand on Melanie's. She felt Melanie's hand tense up in surprise for a moment.

"I'm happy when you're with me," Melanie said in her frank way.

Violet smiled, and this time she didn't look away. Maybe it was all the wine, maybe it was the love, maybe it was the strong mixture of both, but Violet replied softly, "I am, too, Melanie. I'm happier now than I have been in a while."

Melanie smiled again, this time her whole face lighting up. She let go of Violet's hand to pour more wine into her cup.

"We drank too much to drive," she observed. "I guess we'll have to stay here until the morning. It's warm enough."

Violet nodded gratefully. "I guess we should do that."

There was no one near them on this part of the beach. In fact, every time Violet had gone to the beach at night to drown out her sorrows, she had come to this pier. No one ever came here. That was because, besides the old spa, there was nothing at all around it. There weren't even tons of houses around, either, or those who did live around the area, did not creep around the beach at night like Violet sometimes did. Probably because they were normal, which Violet was not.

"I hope we don't look too weird," said Melanie, as if she was thinking Violet's thoughts.

Violet shrugged. "Who cares what we look like? There's nobody here."

Melanie looked over at her, her torso bending in her direction. "You're right, Violet. Who cares?"

Violet felt her heart beating wildly inside of her chest. Both girls were tipsy at this point, but sober enough to understand the complexities of what was happening to them emotionally. Violet, letting the wine and her urges take over, placed her hand on top of Melanie's again- only this time, Melanie's hand was on her thigh.

Feeling a bit of the soft skin of Melanie's thighs was enough to paralyze Violet. She became even more motionless when Melanie wiggled her hand out and, instead, placed it on Violet's so that her hand was only on her thigh.

Violet took a deep breath, feeling a pulsing sensation run through her body that she hadn't felt in literal years. When she-

"You're really consumed with that story, aren't you?" Richie asks me as I stare at my computer with my mouth open.

"Huh?" I am totally caught off-guard.

Richie just shakes his head at me and takes off his shirt to get changed for bed. I realize how late it is and regretfully walk away from the laptop. I am dying to know what happens between Violet and Melanie, but I also want to honor the promise I made to Charli to read it slowly and carefully. To do this, I need to read this when I'm wide awake.

"You are really invested in that story," says Richie, shaking his head. "Give it a break for a while, won't you?"

I shake my head in frustration. "I'm a beta-reader, Richie. I know that doesn't mean anything to you, but it is my job to read her book and give her pointers. It's just taking a little time, that's all."

"You're acting distant," Richie comments as I get into bed. "You've been like this for over a week now, ever since this whole thing started."

I soften. He isn't wrong. "How about we go somewhere this weekend? Maybe out to lunch, or bowling? I know you've been wanting to do that."

Richie gives me a quizzical look. "Could you sound any less thrilled?"

"Ugh," I say. "I'm trying here! You were the one that said you wanted to go bowling. I was just saying we can go this weekend. Look, I know this book is taking up a lot of time. Let's just make the weekend about us, ok?"

"Ok," he says, and I breathe a sigh of relief. Then, he looks at me and says, "You forgot to do the laundry this week."

Although he is right, I have forgotten, his words annoy me. Afterall, I was always doing chores. Why couldn't he see that?

"Ok, I forget to do the laundry once," I say, my teeth gritted. "Maybe you should have done it yourself then, if you needed it done so bad."

Richie sighs. "I just don't want that book to make you forget about your actual life, Kate."

I don't even look at him. Instead, I turn towards the wall and say, "Whatever, Richie. Goodnight."

The next day, I obviously can't wait to read more of *The Hummingbird*. First though, since it's finally the weekend, I have to get through a bunch of errands. Richie drags me to his mother's house where he uselessly attempts to fix her old-school radio from the 70's, and I politely pretend to be interested in all of his mother's creepy porcelain dolls. However, all I can think of is Violet's hand on Melanie's thigh.

I ask Richie if he'd like to go bowling, but he states he is too tired. I can tell by his facial expression that he is frustrated with me and that this is his way of punishing me- by being difficult. I won't let him see that it's getting to me though and so I say nothing.

After stopping at four different stores to grab food and other essentials, I am exhausted when I get home. At nearly thirty-three, although still ridiculously young, my body isn't quite like it was when I was twenty-five.

"I'm gonna watch the game," Richie mutters as he walks away.

I can tell he's pissed. Afterall, I've been more seduced by Charli's novel than by him. Yet, I don't care. At least not at that moment.

Richie and I have already been having some rough times. We have been arguing more and more about little things, and he has been getting on my last nerve about wanting to be a musician. Although I will never be the one to crush his dreams, Richie started talking about moving to Tennessee to be a country singer and get his big break. I told him that he isn't Taylor Swift and "Needs to Calm Down." He didn't really like that comment much, and it had put a barrier between us.

As much as I try to support my husband in everything that he does, his quest for fame is really beginning to annoy me. Especially considering he hasn't once mentioned how I might feel about such a move.

"Alright, hon," I say to him. "I'm going to relax in bed."

"You're going to read that damn book, aren't you?" he asks this in such an accusatory tone that I immediately heat up with anger.

"You know what, go watch your game, Richie," I say with a wave of my hand. "Yes, I'll be reading the book. I promised Charli I would read it. She's counting on me to give her my honest opinion. I can't just ignore it. Deal with it."

Richie huffs and puffs before he shrugs his shoulders, says "fuck it," and then leaves the kitchen.

I put the groceries away as quickly as my arms and hands can do it and then practically run up the stairs. I need to know what happens next.

As I open my laptop, I see a Facebook message from Charli. My heart skips a beat, and I am becoming nervous that she is reading my book and is about to tell me that she hates it. Instead, her message says, "OMG! Your book- it's amazing! I'm learning so much from reading it. Your writing style is beautiful."

I smile, satisfied and flattered. "So is yours!! I'm taking my time with it, which is why I haven't given you my feedback yet. I have hardly been able to put it down!! I absolutely love it so far. I love the way you make your characters seem so real."

"I love that we can learn from each other!" Charli writes back. "I'm so glad you like it so far."

My blood feels hot in my body, like I'm burning from the inside out. I wonder why it feels this way. It must be the excitement of reading a good book. Yes, that was *definitely* it. The book was good. Of course, that was it. What else could it be?

"I'm so excited to see what happens," I write eagerly.

"And I'm excited to read yours, too," she writes. "I'm going to take my time with it also."

I smile to myself and exit the browser, bringing her novel up. I lean back into my bed and adjust it so that that my laptop perfectly aligns with how I'm sitting and place a pillow underneath it. Now, I can relax in peace. I know Richie's game is going to be hours, as he is always so transfixed watching that crap, so I have the time to soak in all of Charli's words like salt in a bathtub.

Violet took a deep breath, feeling a pulsing sensation run through her body that she hadn't felt in literal years. When she began to stroke the top of Melanie's thigh, she felt Melanie's whole body tense. Violet was going to take her hand off, afraid she had upset Melanie, but as she did so, Melanie took her hand and placed it more firmly on her thigh, a bit higher than it was before.

Violet breathed in sharply. She felt a desire emerge in her that seemed to be overtaking her mind completely as *Lust for Life* by Lana Del Rey and The Weeknd played on ironically in the background. Coincidentally, the song happened to be one of the sexiest songs Violet had ever heard, and it went perfectly with the ocean, the wine, and how badly she wanted to do what the song was demanding the lover do.

Take off, take off all your clothes, Lana sang, The Weeknd echoing her thoughts.

When Violet had the courage to look over, she noticed that Melanie's eyes were closed as if she was in a dream. When she opened them, she looked over at Violet in an expression Violet had never seen from her before- a very solemn, serious expression that contradicted her typical light-heartedness.

Suddenly, Melanie reached out her arm and took Violet's hand. Then, leaning her body over, she moved her hand to Violet's face. Violet couldn't help but be mesmerized, both at the surprising feelings she was experiencing, but also by the way Melanie continued to look at her- like a very serious piece of artwork hanging in some famous museum somewhere.

Before Violet could process this or stop herself, she reached behind Melanie's head and brought her face closer. Melanie continued to stare into her eyes, now looking a bit surprised. Violet moved her own face closer to hers. For a moment, just their noses touched softly, the sound of the waves splashing onto the sandy ground and overcoming the song. Melanie slowly brought her lips to hers, first pausing to gently brush her bottom lip before grabbing Violet's back and pulling her closer so that their lips were pressed together, their tongues beginning to dance in each other's mouths.

Violet reached over to softly touch Melanie's face. As they kissed, each one deeper than the last, Violet found herself gently pushing Melanie down so that she was lying on her back on the blanket. Melanie, typically the one full of boldness, looked very submissive like that, with a countenance of both obedience but also impatience.

Suddenly, as if she couldn't stand it any longer, Melanie pulled Violet towards her so that Violet was directly on top of her. They continued to kiss, their hands in each other's hair and their bodies pressed together in a heated passion. Violet felt her whole body tremble as she moved her hand along the side of Melanie's waist, the sensation of her smooth, perfect skin making her feel drunk- and not from the wine. Melanie squeezed Violet's back and turned her head, letting Violet nibble on her neck. When Melanie moaned softly, Violet's body heated up even more and she moved her hand downward.

Melanie gently, almost precariously, lifted herself up on her arms so that she could take her shorts off. Then, she helped Violet slip off her sundress, so slowly that it was almost maddening. Melanie grabbed the opposite side of the blanket, covering both of them up so that they were fully underneath of it. Then, they helped each other take off the rest of each other's clothes, all while hungrily kissing each other. Violet had never kissed anyone like that before, and they continued to kiss as if they were drowning and their mouths held oxygen.

Melanie slowly guided Violet's hand further up her thigh. Violet continued trailing her fingers up, listening to the sound of Melanie's breath getting hallower. Hearing Melanie cry out only made Violet's desire grow inside of her. After some time, Melanie reached out towards Violet, and Violet guided her hand up her own thigh.

Violet's body shook with pleasure, and she could hear unfamiliar cries coming out of her own mouth. Melanie pulled Violet's body towards her and lifted her hips to meet her. Violet could feel herself trembling. She had never experienced desire that intense in her entire life as they moved with each other in a gentle yet impatient dance.

And, that night, underneath the blanket on the beach, Violet was revived.

I close the laptop almost too forcefully. I am too shocked to read any further.

I am feeling increasingly uncomfortable, but it's not because I don't like reading about the sex. Actually, it's for the exact opposite reason, although I tell myself it isn't.

I slowly undress and get changed into my nightgown. I catch myself in the mirror and stare at myself. I can see my breasts peeking out, as the nightgown is sheer, and my hair looks even more red in contrast with the white of it. I frown at the little freckles all over my face and how awkwardly tall I am. I'm still much too thin, and I can see my bones sticking out from my knees. Although I've been told by many people that I'm pretty, I can never seem to believe them no matter how much they tell me.

I momentarily wonder if Charli ever looks at my pictures on Facebook and thinks I'm pretty, too.

I shake off this thought and decide to turn in early. Texting Richie, I write, "Going to bed. Remember to change Lila's water bowl." I know he'll just be watching the game forever, so it will be me alone in the room for God knows how long.

I browse lazily through TikTok, watching silly videos of dogs disobeying their owners, before attaching my phone to the charger. Laying down, I close my eyes; however, I cannot sleep. Instead, I am thinking of Violet and Melanie and their blossoming love story. I can picture the characters perfectly in my mind- the two girls underneath a blanket on the shore as the waves crash down in front of them, both of them freeing themselves to love each other as they please.

I breathe in deeply, suddenly feeling very warm. I sit up and throw my nightgown off before laying back down, feeling a bit cooler. I close my eyes and try to think of how boring work is, or how fucked the government is, or just about anything else besides Charli's story and her words that spill off the pages like a waterfall. But I can't. And the more I try not to think about it, the more I do.

Chapter 4

Work is a bore, as usual. Sometimes I find it hard to believe that I, with such a big imagination, am stuck in such a prison. It seems so unjustly disappointing.

Work does, however, take my mind off of Melanie and Violet's story for a while. Manny, my friend and favorite coworker, comes in and starts complaining about our boss, and he has me laughing for a long time. After this, though, work dies down. I have time to read but, instead of doing that, I look at pretty stationery on Pinterest. I can't read this kind of story at work. If I were to do that, it would be difficult for me to get through the day without going crazy.

When I leave for the day, Manny comes up to me and says, "You look so happy this week! What's going on? Richie finally doing the job right?"

I laugh. Manny is the only person at work that I discuss my personal life with, including my sex life.

"No," I answer with a roll of my eyes. "He still dreams of being a country music star in Tennessee."

Manny laughs in that high-pitched, loud way he always does. "Alright, honey, but still… you look damn happier recently. Are you having an affair?"

I know he is joking, but it makes me feel uncomfortable for a moment, as if he figured out a secret, although this is obviously not the case.

I force a laugh out of my mouth. "I wish," I tease. He laughs again and we wave goodbye as we reach our cars.

"See ya later, bitch!" he says while blowing a kiss at me.

I pretend to grab it and air-kiss him back, as we always do. "Let's get drinks soon. I'm dying to get out of the damn house and this fucking bank."

"Let's do it, honey," Manny agrees, stepping into his fancy Tesla.

I climb into my own 2016 Ford Focus. I take a deep breath and adjust my sunglasses on my face before connecting my Spotify to the Bluetooth. It seems that every single song I play has something to do with sex and intimacy, so I keep skipping the songs until I get to a neutral Katy Perry song. Now, I can drive in peace.

When I arrive home, Richie staying late at work, I force myself to do some house cleaning. It is the only thing that can bore any potent desire right out of me.

Once the cleaning finally calms me down, I bring up my laptop. My body immediately tenses when I see Charli's message.

Charli: "Still reading- about halfway through- it's absolutely fantastic, Kate!"

I smile with satisfaction. She likes it. Charli Diaz actually *likes* my book. This thought excites me more than I want to admit. I am suddenly twenty-years-old again, and I am eager to catch even a glimpse of the captivating author. Twelve years later and I still feel thrilled when I think of her. But now, it seems different than it was back then. Back then, I just simply admired the woman as a much older, published author. And, although I still do, it seems to be in a very different way than it was before.

I am momentarily reminded of a time in high school when I made out with my best friend. We had both been drinking, and I had told her I was in love with her. It wasn't love at sixteen, but it *was* a deep crush. Later, we both laughed about it and chalked it up to the fact that we were both super drunk.

But then there was that time at college. I had been completely sober and watching a movie with my best friend, Elena. We were under the covers, laughing at a funny scene, and our arms touched. It was so innocent, but I remember feeling electrified by the sensation of her skin on mine. It scared me when I desperately wanted her to hold me close to her. She didn't, of course, and I was bitterly disappointed.

In both of those situations, I had been attracted to girls. I never really thought about it, though. I blamed the alcohol for the first time, and the second time I chalked it up to a weird, random outlier. I had never really dated until I met Richie during a college party my senior year. I thought he was funny, and he was very nice to me. He made me feel like I was always the only girl in the room. I liked him immediately, and we got married in only two years after meeting each other.

Now, though, I wonder if I made the right decision…

I am desperate to read more about Violet and Melanie, so I snuggle on the couch with a blanket, Lila purring next to me, and I become immersed into their world once again.

When she woke up, Violet momentarily forgot where she was. She stuck her head out of the blanket, heard the waves and the seagulls, and remembered the night before. However, there was no Melanie lying next to her.

Alarmed, Violet got up and threw her dress on under the blanket. When she looked around and to the left, there was Melanie, dancing gracefully in the wet sand and letting her feet splash the water into the air, only wearing a bra and underwear.

Violet's eyes and head hurt a bit, but she had been able to sleep somehow. Carefully and feeling very sheepish, Violet slowly made her way towards Melanie. When Melanie spun around and saw her, she happily ran up to her.

"Hey! Good morning!" she said cheerfully. "I guess we slept here all night. We should go get some breakfast."

Violet was amazed. It was as if nothing had happened at all. Did Melanie forget?

"Are you alright?" asked Violet softly.

"Why wouldn't I be?" was Melanie's practical answer. Then, looking over at her, she added, "Last night was nice."

"Yes. Nice," Violet replied, unsure of what to say. "Melanie, do you remember…? Well, do you remember what happened between us?"

"Something happened?" Melanie's eyes widened. Then, she began laughing. "Of course, I remember, Violet. How could I forget it?"

Violet wasn't sure if she should be relieved or humiliated.

"Anyway, I'm really hungry. We should get breakfast," Melanie repeated.

Violet nodded and the girls walked back over to the blanket.

"We only drank a bottle," Melanie said with a laugh. "Between the both of us, that wasn't too bad."

What Violet really wanted to say was that she had had the time of her life the night before, wanted to do it again, and was falling helplessly in love with Melanie. Instead, she nodded and replied, "Hmm."

Melanie looked over and gave her a sultry smile that she had never given her before.

"I'd say let's go to my cousin's house," said Melanie, "but Danny has his girlfriend over. I hate that bitch. She's the most uptight person I've ever met in my life."

Violet tried to smile but felt so confused. Did Melanie really enjoy the night? Was she secretly regretting it? Did she have feelings for Violet, too, or was she just having fun?

"I had more than fun," said Violet suddenly. Melanie looked over at her, surprised. "It was more than just nice for me. Last night. It was…it meant more to me than 'nice.'"

Violet's hands were trembling, and her voice was shaking, but she had to know. She had to know if Melanie felt the same way.

Melanie's smile turned into a frown, making Violet's stomach drop violently. Then, she moved closer to Violet, took her hands in hers, and said, "It meant more to me, too. It was more than just nice."

Violet couldn't help but smile. Melanie loved her, too.

Melanie leaned over and kissed her, full and heavy. Violet grabbed her head and kissed her back, leaning into her, her heart dissolving like a bath bomb.

When they drew apart, Melanie reaching out to hold her hand, they retrieved the blanket and Violet's handbag, throwing in the plastic wine cups, and headed back to their cars.

Violet was nervous, but she made the suggestion anyway. "Melanie- did you want to come back to my place? I have waffle mix and fruit salad."

Melanie smiled brightly. "Of course, I would."

Violet breathed a sigh of relief. "It isn't much of a house, though. In fact, it's really more of a shack. It's nothing very nice."

"I don't give a fuck," was Melanie's answer. "Text me your address and I'll Waze it. I'll see you there soon!"

When Violet stepped into her car, she was overwhelmed with a sense of nervousness. What would Melanie think of her little run-down house? Sure, it was only one street away from the beach, and Violet had to sacrifice both of her lungs to afford the house, but it was tiny, cramped, and stuffed with art supplies. What would Melanie think of her then?

"This is so cute!" Melanie said as she entered Violet's house. "You said you lived in a shack, but this is no shack. It's adorable. And the way you've decorated the place is so artsy! I love all the pictures. Did you paint them?"

Violet nodded proudly. She wasn't a proud person, but if she was proud of anything it would be her art.

She watched Melanie walk over to the walls to look up at all the paintings. She stopped when she saw the painting Violet had made of her dog years ago.

Violet laughed. "That's Spotty. He died a few years ago."

Melanie's eyes immediately filled with tears. "I had a dog, too. He died last year, and I haven't been the same. This picture is so lifelike."

Violet nodded gratefully.

"Losing an animal is the hardest thing in the world," said Violet. "I was devastated when Spotty got cancer. He was only five. He was taken from me way too soon."

Melanie looked over at Violet and moved closer, taking her hands. "You are a brilliant artist. I want to see every single thing you have ever done."

Violet laughed. "That's sweet, but that would take a long time. All my childhood stuff is at my mom's in Connecticut, and I've thrown much of my artwork out through the years."

Melanie's face crumbled before her. "How could you throw anything out? Your work is mind-blowing!"

Violet shrugged and walked over a few feet to the little kitchen, grabbing the bag of waffle mix and pouring it into a bowl. Melanie followed her, read the box, and started gathering more ingredients from the fridge. Most people would have found it rude, but Violet loved that Melanie felt so at home around her that she could just open the fridge without asking.

They mixed the ingredients together silently. It wasn't an awkward silence, as Melanie kept laughing at her own little mistakes, and before they knew it, waffles were on the table with a bowl of fruit salad sitting next to them.

"I feel like I'm in a different world in here," Melanie commented, sipping her water. "With all the artwork and the blue walls and the glass figures and seashell decorations…it's like I'm in an underwater paradise!"

Violet giggled and stared at her plate.

"When I was just a kid, I used to want to be a mermaid when I grew up," Melanie said with a laugh. "That's all I'd ask for, for Christmas- for Santa to give me a mermaid tail and make it so I could breathe under water!" Suddenly, a dark look shadowed across her perfect face. "My dad tried his best. He even bought me a fake mermaid tail and swam with me in the pool. He even called me his 'Little Mermaid.' I was obsessed with the movie, too."

Violet, remembering that her father had died when Melanie was young, couldn't help but reach for her hand.

Melanie smiled sadly. "He really was the best dad. Since my mom was addicted to drugs, I went to live with her parents- my grandparents. They hated my dad and wouldn't ever let me talk about him. That was the hardest part. I had to keep quiet around my own family and pretend like my dad didn't even exist."

Violet could feel tears coming into her eyes. "Melanie, I- I'm so sorry. That wasn't ok."

"I know," sighed Melanie, taking another bite out of her waffle. "My grandparents were not the best caretakers emotionally. But they did get me through middle school and high school, so I'll give them that. What about your parents? What are they like?"

Violet shuddered. She hated this question.

"They're alright, I guess," she said. "They both drive me nuts! My dad was ok when I was a kid, but he left us when I was a sophomore in high school, and I haven't seen him since. He does text me every once in a while, though." She watched as Melanie's eyes grew big. "My mom drives me nuts. She has Bipolar Disorder and living with her was...well, not the most fun. I was always being yelled at, and she used to make me sit in the attic for hours if I made a mistake- even if I got a B in school."

Melanie looked genuinely shocked. "Oh my God. That's terrible, Violet. I'm sorry you went through that."

Violet shrugged and took a sip of water. Wanting to change the subject, she said, "What is something you've always wanted to do, Melanie? Something you've wanted to do your whole life?"

Melanie's face brightened and her multi-colored eyes sparkled. "This is so silly, but I've always wanted to go on an African safari! I know it's dangerous and dirty, but I love the idea. I'm going to do it someday. Wait and see."

"I believe you," said Violet with a laugh. If there was one thing she had learned about Melanie, it was that she did what she set out to do and didn't let anything hold her back.

Melanie took a deep breath and put her head in her hands, staring at Violet like she was the greatest thing she had ever seen. It made Violet feel a bit awkward, but also special and important. She had never felt special or important with anyone before.

"Did you want to catch a movie today?" asked Melanie cheerfully. "We can't say we're officially dating unless we see a movie, of course."

This made Violet laugh. "The movies…wow, it's been a while since I've been to the theaters. Sure. Why not? What did you want to see?"

Melanie smiled. "I'll see just about anything. I love a good action film- all the gore and blood makes me excited! I know that sounded weird. But I like a good romcom, too! I don't like horror movies because they scare me. I know that's kind of lame."

"It's not," assured Violet. "I hate horror movies. I'm not big on action, but romcoms are my favorite. What about the new one, the one where the girl travels in time? I forget what it's called."

"*Time Capsule*!" said Melanie. "Yes! Let's see it!"

After breakfast, the girls looked up the movie times and caught the next film. Violet could not concentrate on the movie the entire time. Having Melanie's hand in hers felt like being in a warm, cozy blanket by the fire in the middle of winter. Melanie radiated warmth and sincerity, and Violet could feel it through her skin.

When the movie was over, they went to a small Italian restaurant to have pizza and chat. Melanie was thrilled with the movie, and talked on and on about how cool it would be to travel to the future. Violet could hardly pay attention. Melanie was so animated and talked with her hands flying in the air, speaking a mile a minute. Her eyes shone and her smile shone even brighter, lighting up the entire restaurant. Even her voice was exciting and bubbly. Violet was completely transfixed by her.

After pizza, Melanie turned to Violet and said, "I guess I should go home now. I don't want you to get sick of me. I like you, Violet."

Violet's heart jumped into her throat. "You don't have to go."

Melanie looked surprised. "I don't want to bother you."

"You're not a bother," said Violet, reaching out for her hand. "Let's go back to my house. We can have some wine- maybe only *one* glass this time," (they both laughed), "and you can tell me all about your life. I want to know everything."

Melanie looked flattered. "Well, ok. As long as you don't mind."

Mind? Violet would have sacrificed a kidney to have Melanie spend another moment with her.

"I'd love it if you came back," said Violet sincerely.

So, she did.

Sitting on the couch with the promised glass of wine in their hands, Melanie turned Lana Del Rey on Spotify before Violet began asking her questions about everything. Violet felt that she needed to know it all. What was her favorite color? Who was her favorite actor or actress? What kind of coffee did she like? What was her middle name? Was she named after anyone in particular? Had she ever witnessed something paranormal? Where had she traveled to so far? What was her dog like? What was her favorite animal? What made her cry? What made her smile? What scared her?

Melanie answered all of these questions in great detail. She didn't have a favorite color, as all colors were good for different things. She also had no favorite actor or actress, as there were so many that she couldn't possibly choose just one- (*The Great Gatsby* movie with Leonardo DiCaprio and Carey Mulligan was one of her favorite movies). Melanie was not much of a coffee drinker, but she did love a pumpkin spiced latte in the fall. Her middle name was "Nicole" and she was named "Melanie" simply because her parents liked the name. She absolutely had witnessed a paranormal event. When she was in high school, she and her friends played with a Ouija board and at one point, it had spelled out, "DEATH BE CLOSE" before the little board piece flew up into the air and hit the wall. Since then, Melanie never touched a Ouija board again.

Melanie loved to travel, and her favorite place so far was Italy. She loved the music, the food, the culture, and all of the excitement, and even had her first real kiss there as a teenager. Her dog, Roger, was a beagle and she loved him with all of her heart. He was an old sixteen years when he passed away, and Melanie cried for him often. He was her best friend and had helped her get through her father's death. This made her cry, along with nearly anything in the news. In fact, Melanie couldn't stand the news, and any bit of negativity would throw off her vibe completely, which is why she stayed away from it whenever she could.

Old movies and old music made her smile along with making crafts and sitting in the sun. She had always been afraid to die before being truly loved, and this had been her greatest fear. Her favorite animal was- interestingly enough- a hummingbird.

When Violet asked why she loved hummingbirds so much, Melanie explained, "Hummingbirds have so many special meanings. They're not only beautiful, but they're more intelligent than most people think."

Melanie went on to explain that she was a descendent of Native Americans on her father's side, and in that culture, hummingbirds symbolized freedom and zest for life. Melanie certainly had a zest for life. Hummingbirds were agile creatures, using their long beaks to seek out nectar, even on days of bad weather. Just like the spirited animal, Melanie could also find the sweet nectar in life despite the hardships she had gone through. And, like a hummingbird, Melanie was beautiful, positive, and peaceful, getting every single thing she could out of life.

Violet just listened, completely mesmerized. She was no longer falling in love with Melanie- she was now *hopelessly* in love with her.

Melanie asked her the same questions, to which Violet gave short answers. It was still so difficult for her to share personal things, and Melanie had been the only person she had told some of those things to.

Suddenly, as they shamelessly poured themselves another glass of wine, Violet sighed.

"Melanie, there's something I want to tell you, but it might change your mind about me."

Melanie giggled. "I don't think so, Violet. As long as you're not a serial killer, I think we're good."

Violet shook her head. "Promise me that you will try not to judge me."

Melanie reached over to hold her hand. "Violet, I promise!"

Taking a deep breath, Violet said, "That day we met on the beach- well, I wasn't planning on coming home. In fact, I was planning to die. I had a bag that was going to help me. I was just about to put the bag over my head when I saw you. You looked so happy, and I didn't want you to see me. You ruined my bad mood," with this she laughed a bit. "Then when you came to talk to me, you spoiled my dark mood entirely! That's when we made plans to go to Sea Gert's."

She watched as Melanie's mouth dropped. She paused a moment before saying softly, "You mean, you were about to kill yourself at the moment you saw me?"

Violet nodded.

Melanie brought her hands to her face and started sobbing into them.

"Oh, Melanie!" said Violet frantically. "I'm so sorry! I shouldn't have told you!"

Melanie looked up and shook her head. "I'm happy you told me. To think of you so sad breaks my heart. It just breaks me to pieces!" She continued to sob, Violet lightly stroking her hair, before adding, "I don't know what I would do if I hadn't met you. I just don't know what I would have done. To not know you is something I can't bear to think about, Violet."

Violet's face softened and a few tears escaped from her own eyes. "Melanie, you saved my life. If you hadn't been there, I wouldn't be here now."

Still crying, Melanie stood up and said, "I need a tissue!"

Violet hurriedly grabbed her one and came back to the couch.

"I'm sorry I'm crying," sniffled Melanie. "I just- I just love you so much."

Violet's breath sharpened. No one had ever told her they loved her before, not like that at least.

Violet took Melanie's head in her hands and kissed her. Then she said, "I love you too, Melanie."

She watched as Melanie's whole face lit up. Winning the heart of Melanie was Violet's greatest accomplishment so far. She couldn't even believe it. Not only did she never picture herself with another woman, but she never thought she would find the real thing. And here it was, right next to her.

"Make love to me again," said Melanie gently.

Violet put her glass on the table and moved to get closer to her. Kissing her mouth and then her neck, Melanie leaned back and closed her eyes. Violet then put her hand to Melanie's face and stroked her cheek before slowly and carefully moving her hand down her body, where she could feel the heat pulsing from her skin.

I want to message Charli immediately. I want to tell her how infatuated I am with this love story she wrote. I want to give her a big hug and ask her what inspired her to write such a story. Had she ever had a Melanie in her life?

Instead, I take a deep breath and put the story away. I am too engrossed in it to pay attention to structure and grammar, which is part of my job as a beta-reader. I turn on the TV and watch a show, but I'm not really paying attention. I'm itching to read the rest of the book, but I know I need to read it at a time where I am not totally distracted by the plot and characters of the story.

A couple of hours later, Richie returns home, and we agree to watch a movie together. Richie loves it, but I hate action movies, so it bores me to pieces. I take that time instead to freak out about Charli reading my own book. What will she think of it? I shudder when I remember the sex scenes in my story. They are pretty graphic, and I am hoping Charli can handle them without seeing me differently or thinking I'm some kind of sex fiend.

After the movie, Richie watches another game and I go upstairs. I'm a bit paranoid now of Charli reading my own book. I pull up my novel on the computer and begin going through it. Now, I notice so many more mistakes that I have not noticed before. I have learned so much already from reading Charli's novel, and I am somewhat ashamed that I cannot write like she can.

My book is so silly in comparison. It is about a young woman who is saved from being hit by a car by a handsome stranger. The two agree to have dinner and they fall in love. Of course, they have lots of sex which I make sure is very strong- after all, sex sells, right? Then, they get into a quarrel about where they want to live and almost break-up. Instead, they decide their love is worth it and they choose a random place on the map and start their lives over.

I feel that my book is very stupid now. It is simply nothing compared to Charli's. It's frivolous and generic and the characters are way overdone. I inwardly regret sending my book to Charli, despite her saying it's amazing. Perhaps she is just being nice.

I get a notification on Facebook and click it.

"Taking my time with your book, Kate," writes Charli. "It's so descriptive!"

I cringe, hoping she isn't talking about my wild sex scenes which were, in fact, extremely descriptive. I am not sure if she means this in a good way or a not-so-good way.

"I'm in love with your book," I write back feverishly. She has to know. "I'm absolutely blown away. I'm also still taking my time. I'm more than halfway finished, but I want it to last. I promise I will give my feedback very soon. I'm enjoying it so much."

I exit out of Facebook, too nervous to see if she replies, and pull up her story. I am once again immersed in Violet and Melanie's world. I read as they go on adventures together- parasailing, rock-climbing, dancing… The two of them do not fail to impress me, and I can't put the damn book down.

Chapter 5

"Violet," said Melanie as they lie together in bed.

"Don't," Violet replied. "Don't remind me that the summer is ending, and you have to return to Pennsylvania. Don't do it. Not today."

"Well, maybe I don't have to," said Melanie with a conspiring grin.

Violet turned over, surprised. "What?"

"Violet, I know we've only been dating for a couple of months, but we love each other. Why should we be apart? I don't want to be apart."

Violet smiled sadly and brushed a piece of Melanie's silky hair out of her face. "I don't even want to think about it. I can't think about it."

"Well, if that's true," said Melanie, now sitting up, "then you'll listen to me. I know I have the teaching job in Pennsylvania, and you know I love the kids, but I can find another job around here. I'm qualified and someone's bound to hire me! Maybe I can ask my cousin if I can live with him until I get a job and can get my own apartment."

Violet was both surprised and touched. "But you always talk about your kids! You love teaching them!"

Melanie nodded. "Yes, I do. But I love you more."

With this, Violet also sat up. "I love that you want to stay here. But I don't think it's a good idea." Melanie's whole face crumbled. Seeing that, Violet said quickly, "You shouldn't live with your cousin. You should live right here with me. In my little shack."

Melanie's eyes lit up once more, and she squealed in excitement. "Are you serious? Really?"

"Of course, I'm serious," said Violet practically. "I usually am, you know that. Melanie, stay with me. Stay here. I know it's not much of a house, but we can get something bigger one day. We can make this our own. You can decorate it in any way you want. I'll even let you have a mermaid theme!"

Melanie began to laugh. "Oh, Violet, of course I will. I will be wherever you are!"

At this, Violet burst into tears.

"Aw, babe!" Melanie cooed, bringing her closer and kissing the top of her head. "I love you so much."

Trying to gain her composure, Violet answered, "I love you, too. More than I can say with words. You continue to save my life over and over again."

With that, Melanie squeezed her tighter. "You make my life worth living, Violet. You really do. I can't wait to move in with you."

A week later, it was Melanie's 30th birthday.

Violet was scrambling to get everything done. She had saved up money and rented a big hotel suite on the water, and invited two of her friends that Melanie had met.

Being Melanie, she had made those friends her own friends, as she was always the most personable and charming one in a room, and they adored her. They were all excited to celebrate Melanie's birthday.

"Ugh, *thirty*!" exclaimed Melanie the morning, her hands to her head. "I can't believe it! I'm so old!"

Violet laughed. "Wait until you hit thirty-five. That's when you really start feeling it."

Melanie laughed and took a spoonful of cereal. "You know, I think I saw my father yesterday."

Violet looked over at her, confused. "What do you mean?"

Melanie leaned her head into her one hand. "A hummingbird came and sat right in front of me on the beach. I've never even seen a hummingbird on the beach here before. Not only were they there, but they also came to me, too. They flew around my face and then stopped by my feet. They came so close to me that I just knew it was my father. In the Native American culture, we believe that hummingbirds can be spirit animals. I think this was my dad saying, 'Happy Birthday' to me."

Violet, always transfixed by whatever Melanie said, walked over to the couch to sit next to her.

"I bet he was, Melanie," said Violet. "I wouldn't be surprised at all."

Melanie smiled sadly. "I just love hummingbirds! I used to collect little hummingbird figurines as a kid. When I moved in with my grandparents, they threw all of them away. It was a sad time for me."

Violet touched her hand. "I'm sorry that happened. I'll buy you back all the hummingbird figurines in the world if you want."

Melanie smiled, this time a happier one. "The thing is I know you would try to do that. You have the kindest heart of anyone I've ever met."

Blushing, Violet shook her head and stood up.

"Come," she said. "Let's get dressed. I know it's going to take you forever. We have the brunch with your cousin and then I'm taking you somewhere special."

Brunch was alright, but it was obvious that Melanie did not want to be there, and she really despised her cousin's girlfriend, who was, as she said, very uptight and snobbish. Melanie didn't pretend to enjoy herself and, afterwards, she said to Violet, "I'm so glad that shit is over."

Violet giggled. "Well, the next thing we have planned is going to be really fun."

"What is it?"

Violet gave her a wink. "You'll see."

When Violet pulled up to the little garden, Melanie looked confused.

"A garden?" she asked. "Hmm. That's interesting!"

Violet stifled laughter and the two girls left the car.

Upon entering, Melanie pointed to a huge relic of a hummingbird on the wall. This delighted her beyond expectation, and she was even more surprised as she walked into the greenhouse garden. For there, flying through the greenery and speckles of sweet-scented flowers, was a bunch of beautiful hummingbirds. They were everywhere- in the little trees, racing through the aisles, sucking nectar from azaleas. It was a gorgeous sight. However, it was not nearly as gorgeous as the look on Melanie's face when she first walked in.

"Oh my God," she said, putting her hands to her mouth in shock. "Violet! Violet! Hummingbirds! I can't believe it! I have never seen so many in one place!"

Violet reached for her hand and smiled. "I thought you'd like it."

"Like it?" Melanie said, tears now streaming down her cheeks. "No. I don't like it. I absolutely love it!"

The girls began walking through the aisles of flowers, hummingbirds racing all around them. Some of the birds had deep red feathers while others had bright pink heads. Some had little green bodies and others had bright wings as purple as irises. Many had feathers of the brightest blue and others looked like they had been painted with gold.

Melanie was totally hypnotized. For several minutes, she was completely quiet. It was very unlike her to say nothing, and, for a moment, Violet was worried. But when she turned around, there was the happiest smile on her face.

"Violet," she said. "I don't have any words for this. I can't believe you even remembered. I was already having a great day, but now- well, now, it's become the best day of my life."

With that said, Violet wrapped her arms around her and held her to her chest.

"I'm glad you love it."

"I could stay here with you forever," said Melanie.

"Me too, my little hummingbird."

And they kissed amidst the wild colors and magnificent creatures.

I smile to myself as I minimize the browser. I am happy for Violet, as I find myself relating to her.

I'm glad she found someone to love and who loves her back.

I think again of my silly story and shake my head.

Why did I let her read it? I say to myself.

I'm so embarrassed to think of her reading my ridiculous sex scenes. Charli wrote hers in such a delicate, careful way. Mine are much wilder and raunchier.

Well, there is nothing I can do about it now.

I walk over to the mirror and stare at myself again. I can't help but feel jealousy. But it's not because of Charli's writing. It's something else that's making me jealous.

As crazy as it is, I realize I am jealous of Melanie- Charli's fake character in her book. The way Charli describes Melanie- so full of life and innocent enthusiasm- is something I can never compare to. Her beauty, her demeaner, all of the things Charli describes her as, are just not me. I am probably nowhere near as pretty as Melanie must be, nor am I as vibrant and full of life. I'm just Kate. Plain old Kate. Charli would never describe me in the beautiful ways she describes Melanie. This thought, despite being irrational, does not sit well with me.

I wonder again if Melanie is a real person. If she is, I think she is very lucky to be loved by someone like Charli. I consider asking Charli if she's based off of someone she knows, but I know that question may be far too personal. At least for now. I will have to get to know Charli a bit better before asking her a question like that.

I hope this will be a door for me to getting to know Charli more. I have always admired her, and it would be an honor to actually be friends with her. It's not something I have ever thought too much about, as she had become an acquaintance. Yet, after beginning to read her writing, my opinion about her is changing. I used to see her as almost this mom-like figure- her being so much older than me- and I felt like a child in her presence. I no longer see her like that. I realize, despite telling myself it's all just simple admiration, it may be more than that. Perhaps I am feeling like Violet did. Perhaps I am developing feelings for someone who has always been a part of my life, but whom I only recently am getting to know.

As much as I try to shake off the thought, it keeps creeping into my mind, making me feel both shame and excitement at the same time.

Chapter 6

"Now, go home and get changed, and we'll meet at the hotel," ordered Violet, putting her hands on Melanie's skinny, tanned shoulders. "I just need to pick up a few things."

Melanie smiled mysteriously. "You better not be buying me too much. The greatest birthday gift is having you to share it with."

Violet winked and playfully pushed her out the door. "Don't worry about it. It's just some small things. Anyway, once we get to the hotel, we can get ready for the nightclub, and then the real fun will start!"

Melanie trailed her finger across Violet's chest and said, "I think once we return to the suite, that will be when the real fun starts."

Violet blushed and leaned over to kiss her. Melanie's lips, so sweet and passion-filled, made Violet get weak in the knees, as usual.

"I'll text you when I'm on my way," said Melanie, her colorful eyes sparkling. "Remember- don't get anything big!"

Violet laughed and rolled her eyes.

When Melanie left, Violet texted her other friends and then got ready. For once, instead of wearing her usual drab clothing, Violet wanted to sparkle. She chose a black dress with sequins around it and matching heels. She placed a gold bracelet and gold earrings on, and was even bold by putting on red lipstick and gray eyeshadow. She hadn't gotten this dressed up in years. She had to admit, she looked pretty good.

Violet then ran out to a couple of stores, grabbing big gold balloons, "30th birthday" decorations, a birthday mug, a birthday hat, and a birthday sash. To Violet's surprise, she was even able to find a beautiful hummingbird figurine at a Hallmark store. Violet hoped it would remind Melanie that she had a bright future, and that Violet would always try to make her happy.

"Remember- nothing big!!" said a text from Melanie.

Violet smiled to herself and texted back, "Sure thing!"

She then headed back into her car to drive to the hotel suite. While on the way, she carelessly put on Lana Del Rey and drove with the windows down, making waves with her hand just like Melanie always did. Melanie's contagious energy had fully seeped into Violet, and Violet had finally let all her colors show.

Arriving at the hotel, Violet met up with their two friends- Abby and Maria- and they started decorating their hotel suite. Violet could not have been more excited. She knew Melanie was just going to love everything about that night. Melanie always appreciated the little things, and she knew that the attention, the friendships, and even the little hummingbird figurine would make those heavenly eyes sparkle and that wide smile break open like a blossoming flower.

"Omw!" texted Melanie. "Be there soon!! Can't wait! Xox! Love you!"

"Drive safe!" Violet texted back. "Love you a million times!!!"

The three girls finally finished decorating, and Abby put the sparklers on the cake, before they all went down to the lobby to sip champagne and wait for Melanie to arrive.

Violet could not have been more excited. Her heart was bouncing in her chest, and she could feel her legs hopping up and down underneath her. Melanie was going to *love* this.

After some time, and three glasses of champagne, Violet sent her a text: "Where you at babe? We're in the lobby! Get ready for some 30th-birthday champagne!"

Melanie must have been stuck in traffic because she didn't text back. Violet, Abby, and Maria talked and laughed about TV shows until Violet began growing worried. It had been an hour since they had arrived at the lobby, and Melanie was 30 minutes away at *most*. Where the hell *was* she?

Violet called her phone but only her cheerful, "Hey! It's Mel!" voice message came on.

"Melanie, call me back asap. Your champagne is getting warm."

After another twenty minutes passed, Violet was now panicking.

"Do you want me to go to her cousin's house to make sure she left?" asked Maria. "Maybe she got stuck there. Her nephew might be talking her ear off."

Violet, glancing at her phone in worry, said, "Ok, but let me try one more time."

She called again. And then again. But Melanie didn't answer.

"Ok, Maria, go check on the house- I'll text you the address," agreed Violet. "I think we'd better call the police, Abby."

Without thinking twice, Abby got out her phone and dialed 911, explaining the situation and that their friend was supposed to be at the hotel an hour ago, and had left an hour and a half ago. Violet, feeling a sick pit of dread in her stomach, could not sit down. She decided to walk outside of the hotel and stand at the doors near the parking lot, looking for any signs of her girlfriend. She even took a cigarette from Abby and began inhaling like it was water, her hands shaking violently. She didn't smoke, but she didn't care at that moment.

Time passed on. It went on and on. Maria had confirmed with Melanie's cousin that she had, indeed, left for the hotel long ago and was not home.

An hour later- after Violet texting and calling Melanie at least forty times- Violet began to cry. Maria arrived back and she and Abby took turns holding Violet as she crumbled in front of them.

Officers were now there, looking around the parking lot and the streets around them. It seemed like hours, but it was only a half hour later when one of the officers who had been chatting with the girls got a call.

"We think we've got her," said the voice on the other line.

The officer hastily walked away so that the girls couldn't hear the conversation. When he came back to them, there was a dark look of complete defeat on his face.

When he paused, Violet knew. She was gone.

"Unfortunately, your friend was in a very bad car accident on the way over here," said the officer, his own voice choking up. "She- she was driving down Arnold Avenue, and someone ran a red light. Ran right into her."

"Which hospital is she at?" asked Abby frantically.

The officer looked at the ground. "I'm so sorry. I'm so sorry but she didn't make it."

Upon hearing this, Violet collapsed. She felt her whole world spinning underneath her feet. She couldn't even feel herself hit the concrete. It was unreal.

She vaguely felt herself being lifted up by her friends, but she could see or hear nothing except muffled voices.

Melanie was gone. Her favorite person in the whole world, the person that meant absolutely everything to her, the girl who saved her life- she was gone.

Everything turned to black as Violet became incapacitated with despair. It was Melanie's birthday, and now she would never have another one.

As Violet continued to scream and sob, Abby, Maria, and the officers got Violet into Abby's car and they drove to the morgue. Violet could not bear to go inside. She just knew in her heart that Melanie would not want her to see her in that state.

No. Melanie would want her to remember her just as she was- smiling, glowing, and full of life. Not bruised and bloody on a cold steel table.

Violet stayed in the car while Abby and Maria gathered some of Melanie's things. Melanie's cousin arrived soon after- a complete mess- to talk more about arrangements. He knew Violet and Melanie were dating, and he was kind enough to ask Violet if she had any special requests.

"The hummingbird," she was able to choke through her tears. "I got her a hummingbird figurine for her birthday. It's at the hotel. Please- I would like her to be buried with it."

"I'll go and get it tomorrow," her cousin promised.

Giving Violet a squeeze on her shoulder, he added, "Melanie was the most awesome girl. She always wanted to find real love. Thank you for loving her."

Violet, in too much shock to respond, closed her eyes and prayed to the Universe that it wasn't true, and that Melanie would be creeping up beside her with her bright smile at any moment, telling her it was all a big joke and that she had got her good. When that didn't happen, Violet stayed over Abby's apartment that night. She couldn't sleep a wink, and the next day, she went back to her little house- this time all alone.

As soon as she walked through the door, she began wailing and screaming, kicking anything in her path and throwing her artwork off of the walls. How could her Melanie be taken so recklessly from her arms? If Violet had gone with her and didn't let her drive alone, maybe none of this would have happened. With that thought, Violet collapsed on the floor, finally falling into an unsettling sleep.

Through Melanie's cousin, Violet was able to help with the funeral arrangements. Melanie's mother responded that she did not care where Melanie was buried and was too busy to be bothered with any of it, so Violet and Danny carried out the entire funeral procession.

They decided she should be buried there, at the Jersey Shore- after all, it was the place she loved most in the world and where she had finally found the love that she was so afraid she would never find. Violet had her wish and made sure that Melanie was buried with her little hummingbird figurine, along with a long note where Violet poured out how much she meant- and would always mean- to her.

How could someone so full of life not be alive anymore?

Later, she (reluctantly) went to lunch with Danny, Abby, Maria, Danny's girlfriend, Danny's kid, and Danny's friend. Of course, Violet couldn't eat. All she did was stare at her plate. She had done nothing but scream and cry for nearly five days now, and she was finally all cried out.

When Violet was dropped back off at her lonely little home, it was so obvious that all the light that had once been there was gone. Now, it was back to being dead, cold, and lifeless- just like Violet felt inside.

Unable to tolerate the silence, Violet angrily took a bottle of pinot grigio from the fridge, got into her car, and drove to the beach. She needed to be near Melanie again. She missed her so much already. How was she supposed to live without her? She couldn't before. So how was she supposed to, now that she knew what being loved by Melanie was like? She couldn't bear it.

Sitting on the beach drinking, Violet stared blankly out into the waves. Just like her sorrow, they kept crashing and crashing, making their way towards her. Violet thought of the moment she was about to put her head in the bag and saw Melanie. The thought of not seeing Melanie and being dead, and never getting to love Melanie, was a thought that was more unbearable than anything she had ever experienced.

"Thank you for letting me love you," Violet said into the air. "My hummingbird. I'm going to miss you more than you know. But I'm not going to do it, Melanie. I'm not going to end myself. You have shown me that life is worth living. It won't mean as much to me now that you're gone, but I know you would want me to keep going. I know you wouldn't be able to handle the thought of me ending my life because of your death. Afterall, you're the reason I'm alive."

And with that, Violet looked over in shock. For there, in all its stunning beauty, was a beautiful hummingbird, flying around her head. They looked into Violet's eyes, a complete look of compassion embedded deep within them, and flew away.

Violet burst into tears but smiled. She knew it was Melanie- she just knew it. And she knew that, in some way or form, her little hummingbird would always be with her forever, all of Melanie's light and love surrounding her throughout her life until it was her time to see her again.

I am too shocked to move. My eyes are too blurry to see. I am completely incapacitated by the ending of this book.

I suddenly burst into tears and close the computer, almost angry at the suffering I am experiencing from this story. I never expected it to end this way. I never expected Melanie's death and the tragic scenes that followed it.

I walk over to the kitchen and pour myself more tea. I can hardly see a thing, as I am still sobbing disgustingly, my whole face dripping with tears and snot.

The book is so touching, so mesmerizing, so engulfing- it took me to another place entirely. I have fallen in love with this beautiful story. And I have also fallen in love with the writer who wrote it.

The next day, I am anxious to write my feedback for Charli. She must know not only how special her story is, but how special *she* is.

I start out by stating a few of the little grammatical things I noticed, which was not very much, and then I talk about how moving the book is, how much I love it, and how much it means to me. I go on and on, pages by pages, giving her a very vivid description of my adoration. It is perhaps a bit too much in terms of praise, but I want Charli to know how amazing it is. Not just that I *think* it is amazing, but that it is actually truly exceptional. She needs to know how much it affected me.

I anticipate her response as I bite my nails. She quickly messages me back.

"I just read your email- oh my goodness! It made me tear up! Thank you so much for your feedback. I'll have yours to you soon!"

My heart sails. I have pleased her. Maybe my own book will sweep her off her feet like hers did to me.

It is two days later, and I am sitting on my couch watching Netflix. I am not feeling the greatest, so I decided to stay home from work today. The thought of sitting at that desk is more than I can bear at the time being. I'm eating cereal, the millennial diet, when I hear a little ping go off on my phone.

Yawning, I pick it up. Oh my God. It's from Charli.

Opening it, my heart drops. It reads:

"Hey! I've had time to read through your book. Thanks for sharing your story with me!!"

I suddenly have a feeling of dread. I don't quite know why, but I have a terrible feeling for some odd reason. I shrug it off, knowing I'm being ridiculous. I scroll through the email and read her suggestions.

I am finished reading in about two minutes. Her suggestions are not what I had anticipated. In fact, they are nothing at all what I expected from such an amazing writer. Her feedback is very brief, very curt, and even a bit condescending.

She clearly hates it, which she makes very obvious by her negative comments and by telling me to essentially change my whole plot. She gives me a couple vague compliments, but they are usually followed by a 'but' at the end. She hardly says one real positive thing about my writing or my book. She also seems to be easily confused over big plot events, and it appears as though she has skimmed it more than actually read it. She only focuses on the first parts of the story, and does not talk about the middle or ending at all. It is quite obvious that she didn't read it and, if she did, I'm an unequivocal failure at writing.

I know my writing is subpar to hers, and I know my story will not be everyone's cup of tea. However, I cannot help but think she could have been a bit nicer in her feedback and perhaps may have said more helpful or constructive things. Not only did she rip it to pieces, but she mentioned giving me feedback based on my "skill level."

What the fuck does *that* mean?

My cheeks grow hot with embarrassment. My eyes fill with tears and my hands begin to shake. I feel completely gutted by her comments. Not only does she hate my book, but she clearly dislikes me enough to not have more than one real positive comment to say about it. It is clear that she got nothing from my story. And, as silly as my story is, I still thought there were some important themes that she may have pointed out. But she didn't. Instead, she ripped up my book along with my heart.

I clutch my chest. I did not expect to be this hurt. I cry into my hands, Lila stepping all over me and wondering why I'm going crazy. I cannot believe this is the feedback I received.

Did I praise her own story too much? Was she freaked out by my praise? Was she just frustrated with me in general? I am not sure why she made such unkind comments about my story and my writing. All I know in this moment is how hurt I feel and how utterly and completely disappointed she has made me.

Chapter 7

When Richie comes home and greets me, I tell him to leave me alone. It is harsh, I know, but just his very presence right now is annoying to me. I feel totally alone in what happened with Charli, and he is the last person on Earth I want to discuss this with. He would never understand. Also, how could I possibly explain to him that I gained feelings for a *woman*? I know that will not go over well. I will have to keep my mouth shut.

I retire to my bedroom. I quickly message Charli, "*Got your feedback- thanks so much!*" She writes back quickly, "*I hope it gives you inspiration!*"

Inside, I am heart-broken. It is clear that not only does she hate my book, but she does not feel the same way about me as I do about her. Otherwise, she could never have said some of the unkind things she stated.

It serves me right. I'm married. I shouldn't have feelings for anyone else, anyway. Yet, I do, and I'm hurt.

I curl up in a ball on my bed and let myself cry for a very long time. When Richie comes up and asks if I've eaten, I say, "I'm too tired to eat. I'm going to bed. Goodnight."

"Ok, well, let me know if you change your mind. Goodnight, hon," he says.

I can tell he's worried, but I have no strength to discuss this with him. At least not now.

I wake up the next morning and go to work in a blur of grief.

Not even Manny can make me laugh today. I am absolutely distraught, and I make little mistakes throughout the day. When work is finally over, I go sit at my favorite coffee house downtown. Usually, I would invite Elena to sit with me, but I am too upset to have company.

I stare out the window, sipping my Frappuccino, and bite my lip. What did Charli hate about my book? What was the worst part of it for her? Why couldn't she point out hardly anything positive about it after already telling me she loved it? What changed for her?

As I sit there and wonder, the feelings of sadness begin to relax. Now, there is another emotion coming up for me- anger.

It hits me like a ton of bricks and I stand up, bang my coffee cup on the table, and head out the door.

I am livid. I cannot remember the last time I was so furious. I am seeing red.

I clench my fists and grit my teeth all the way home. When I get there, I run into the living room and throw a pillow at the ground, yelling into the air.

Lila is clearly confused, as she runs and hides under the couch. She has never seen me so manic before.

Charli has screwed me over and I am *pissed*.

Hastily, without thinking, I pull up my computer. I'm going to tell this woman how I really think this went down.

"Hey there," I write sarcastically. *"I just wanted to tell you that I did not find your feedback inspiring. In fact, I found it overwhelming. I told you in my feedback that I felt lucky to know you, and then you give me this? WTF? Clearly, you dislike me so much that you didn't even read the book. I am not that stupid. Do you think I'm an idiot? I can tell you skimmed it. Your comments on the plot made no sense. You might as well have just told me to 'change the entire story.' The comments were not helpful in the slightest bit. You clearly got nothing out of it. Ouch. If you actually did read it, I'm not a very effective writer and I should rethink my writing career.*

I think there are some things you need to know about your book. I was biased and in a rose-colored cloud of admiration the last time I gave you my feedback. I'm not biased anymore.

First of all, Violet is so annoying and cringey. Her actions don't make much sense in the plot, and I couldn't help but despise this character and her pity-party. Melanie herself is not much better. She's melodramatic, very silly, and so cheerful that she's unrealistic. You did a lackluster job at describing

Violet's depression, as you don't continue to mention it throughout the story. Also, her obsession with Melanie borderlines creepy to be honest with you. Melanie's death could have been better written, and I honestly can't stand the way you write their love story.

So, no. I didn't find your feedback helpful. In fact, I found it meaningless. I was also biased, like I said before. Was it my praise that made you pissed? Were you uncomfortable with the sex? Sex sells, whether or not it makes you uncomfortable. I don't care about what you think of my story. Just delete it from your computer. I have already deleted yours. And don't worry about responding. I can't imagine how pissed off you are at me now and I have no energy to argue back and forth. With that, have a great day!"

I slam the computer shut and sob into my hands. I know what I just said was pretty horrible, but I don't care. I also know that what I said about her story was simply not true, but I am pulsing with hot anger and my blood is boiling.

I go on my phone and browse through stupid TikTok's until I see her response.

"SO sorry you had that reaction. I gave you feedback that I thought could help evolve your writing. I did not anticipate that you weren't ready to manage it. I tried to say that you're a really good writer! I didn't point out all the good things about your book because I was trying to give you constructive

feedback. Again, I didn't know you were not ready to handle that. For this, I apologize."

I stare at the response, my eyes wide. If I was angry before, I am enraged now.

Ready to handle that? Again, what the *fuck*?

In a heated frazzle, I write back, *"You didn't address any of the concerns I just asked you about. Nothing about what you said was even constructive. You don't get to be dismissive and entitled just because you're a published author. I'm published too, but I didn't throw it in your face. I've wanted to be a writer my entire life and I'll never stop writing now. I am not sure why you so clearly dislike me or what I did to make you hate me so much. Do you have feelings for me? Is that why you're angry with me? You didn't treat me like a friend or an equal in this situation. Either way, I hope the next time you see a hummingbird, you think of me and how I'm going to fly despite you trying to clip my wings."*

I throw my phone across the couch and continue to cry. I am humiliated, infuriated, and also degraded. She had ripped my story apart. Cleary, she hates me, my writing, and my book, and regrets sharing our stories now.

I listen to my "Fuck It" playlist on Spotify, pumping myself up to feel even angrier than I already am, and then I call Elena and bitch about it.

Elena helps me calm down a bit and I am finally able to put something in my stomach.

When Richie gets home, I immediately leave the house to go to the park. I need to clear my head and I absolutely cannot do that in that god-forsaken house.

As I walk and listen to *Rage Against the Machine*, I suddenly have a sick feeling in the pit of my stomach. I swallow and distract myself with the angry lyrics of the song, but now I am feeling another emotion- regret.

I sit on the park bench and contemplate what has happened. Yes, Charli had crushed my emotions and was not very nice about her feedback on my story. However, I said pretty shitty, really awful things. Perhaps, although she had hurt my feelings, it was not ok to say these spiteful things to her. Maybe I have royally fucked up.

I reread her feedback and then my responses to it. The more I think about it, the more humiliated I am. Her feedback wasn't the greatest, and it makes sense that I would be angry and hurt by it. Yet, I retaliated in a way that was exceptionally cutting. I did not only express frustration and anger in my response, but I had insulted her, too. I had gone way overboard. I had disrespected her book and her character.

I start to cry again, but this time it isn't from rage. This time, I realize what I have done.

"You have to stop crying," says Richie as he attempts to comfort me on our couch. "She was a bitch. You responded back. Who cares?"

He could not know the extent of how much *actually* care.

I shrug and say, "I feel bad about the things I said. I went overboard, Richie. I didn't have to go where I went. I went too far. I was just so *angry*!"

Richie rubs my back, but I recoil away. I don't want him touching me. For some reason, I have been so resentful of him. I don't even know why.

"What did *I* do?" he asks defensively.

I sigh. It isn't his fault I fell in love with a woman. It isn't his fault that I may not actually be straight and living a lie as a heterosexual my whole life. Suddenly, I am swept up in a grief for him, too.

"I'm so sorry," I say, my head in his chest. "I'm so sorry, Richie."

His voice softens as he holds me close. "Sorry for what?"

I shrug. I don't even know what to say. All I know is that I can never tell him my secret- that not only have I fallen for someone else, but for a woman.

The next day I am in a complete panic. I realize now that the things I said were spiteful and cruel. Despite feeling slighted, it did not give me an excuse to behave like a petulant child. I realize that I just ruined a professional relationship with my favorite author. I *have* to find some way to fix it.

I write her on both Facebook and her email, so that I make sure she reads it.

"Dear Mrs. Diaz," (I no longer feel I have the right to address her by her first name- not after the rude things I said),

"I am SO very sorry for my reaction to your feedback. I'm going to get therapy to process my reaction to this. I felt that I took a lot of time with your book and felt you didn't really read mine. I felt your feedback was mainly negative and it hurt my feelings because I cared about your opinion. I had no right to say such awful things or behave like that. I am SO beyond sorry. I ruined everything. Please forgive me."

A few minutes later, she writes back, "I'm glad you're going to therapy to process the reaction. It's not ruined- only something to be learned from."

"I feel horrible, I am really so sorry," I write back frantically.

She puts a thumbs up to my message and I cringe. I need to fix this somehow, in some way.

I click on a new browser and immediately go searching online for a hummingbird figurine. I don't know how else to fix this. Perhaps if I send her something, she'll know how much I care and how sorry I am.

After much searching, I think I find a really nice one. It's a blue and green crystal hummingbird with a pink neck. It is highly priced, but affordable enough, and I don't think twice when paying for it and sending it right to her house, as she put her address on the front page of her story.

Worried that she may be creeped out by that, I hastily message her, *"I wanted to let you know that I sent you something in the mail as a thank you for reading my book. I'm so sorry again for everything. I'm going to grow from this experience."*

She does not respond, although I can see that she has seen it. I am inwardly panicking to a point where I'm shaking. Perhaps she needs to know how I really feel. Maybe that is the only way she will ever forgive me for what I have said.

I pull up her messenger again and type, *"I have to be honest with you. The reason why I freaked out was because I care for you too much. I developed feelings for you, which is so inappropriate for so many reasons. I hope you are not too angry with me. I didn't intend on this happening at all, and I'm so sorry. Please forgive me."*

Later, I see that she has seen it, as her little profile bubble pops up on my message. She has not responded, and I can only pray she forgives me once she sees how beautiful the figurine I sent her is.

After sending yet again another more detailed apology letter, full of remorse and regret, I wait. In my mind, though, I know I have completely fucked up and ruined all chances to be her friend. I know that I have done something irreparable that no amount of hummingbird figurines is going to fix.

Chapter 8

A week goes by. A miserable week, at that. I cannot stop crying, and Richie is growing concerned. All I can think about is how much I hurt Charli. I picture her getting the last nasty message and what she was probably thinking and feeling. What a horrible person I am.

In a last-ditch effort to obtain her forgiveness, I write one more letter to her on Facebook and email.

"I'm not handling what happened well at all and I'm really sad. I'm sorry that, despite telling you I'll stop bothering you, I keep bothering you. I can say sorry a million times, but I feel those words say very little. I wish there was something I could do to make it up to you, but there's nothing. I don't want to push, but I would appreciate it if we could talk. Even if you tell me to go to hell, I'd prefer that over nothing. Please, give me everything you disliked about my book, or me, or my behavior. I won't freak out this time and I don't care if it's hard to hear. You can tell me the truth. I really loved your story- the things I said were not true. It's very rare to find someone who can take normal life experiences and craft them in a way that evokes magic, but you can. Before you start querying, you need to know that the story is beautiful and you should be really proud of it, and yourself. When I think of hummingbirds now, I think of you and your positive energy. We reached out to each other for a reason, and I refuse to believe it was only for this reason. I don't believe we both

finished our books at the same time out of nowhere or by coincidence. I think it was supposed to bring us together as friends. I sound crazy but you already think I'm crazy, so it does nothing. Please don't feel like you have to respond today or right now, but I'd appreciate it if you could think about talking soon.

-Kate"

I nervously shut my laptop and stare out the window for twenty minutes. I am so anxious I can barely breathe. In what seems like a very short time, I receive a response back from Charli in my emails. Because she wrote back so quickly, I know it's going to be bad.

"Kate,

I have tried not to engage, but clearly, that isn't working. I am now forced to respond to your multiple messages.

I would not define our interactions as friendship. We came to know each other many years ago when I visited your college to speak. I helped you with a manuscript you were working on. That was the extent of our professional relationship. If it was not for you liking some of my posts about writing, we never would have had a reason to interact with each other.

Regarding the sharing of our work- our works are completely separate. It was only a coincidence that we finished our drafts at the same time. I did not just ask you to be a beta-reader, but four other people as well. Each time you message me, you tell me it will be the last, yet- here we go again- another email from you.

I am going to make this very clear to you so that you once and for all understand where I stand- I DO NOT want to talk to you any longer. Although I have tried to have understanding since you're young, I will not hesitate to contact the police or reach out to your husband if I feel like you are threatening me, my family, or my property in any way.

I'm sorry it has come to this, but you forced me to do it. I wish you the best.

-Charli"

I am too shocked to even process the message. I did not expect a response if anything, but this was so much worse than I could have ever imagined it being. I feel completely eviscerated.

Shakily, I walk out of the room, down the stairs, and to the bottle of wine sitting in the cabinet. I pop it open and don't even bother pouring it into a cup. Instead, I just drink straight from the bottle. I go and I go, and I go until the pain is somewhat tolerable and my body feels numb. I know Richie isn't going to be very happy with me, but, at that moment, I do not care. I feel like I just fell through a crack in the earth, and I am spiraling.

When Richie comes home, the bottle is empty and I'm sitting on the floor laughing to myself over how miserable my life has become.

"What the fuck, Kate?" he asks as he lifts me off the floor. Looking over at the empty bottle, he shakes his head. "The whole bottle. Really?"

I continue to laugh. If I don't laugh, I will cry, and then I will never stop.

"I'm putting you to bed," Richie says with a grunt as he carries me up the stairs. I cannot stop laughing. She actually threatened the police on me! How absurd! The situation strikes me as hilarious in this moment, although my heart is shattered to pieces.

I pass out almost immediately when Richie puts me to bed.

The weekend drags on slowly, and I attempt to make myself feel better by going out for coffee with Elena.

"I know I went too far," I say, sipping my latte. "The comments went overboard."

"You did," Elena agrees. "But you apologized multiple times. How many times did she want you to beg for her forgiveness?"

"That's true," I say, feeling a bit of the old spite coming back to me. It makes me calmer, as spite is better than the guilt I have been experiencing.

"Elena, there's more to the story," I say, shaking my head. I bite my lip. There is something I have not told anyone else, but I need to get this off my chest.

Elena gives me a suspicious look before gulping down her second cup of coffee.

"I developed feelings for her," I say quietly. "I know, I know. It's so wrong and inappropriate. For multiple reasons. Her book was just- well, beautiful, and the way she writes is so captivating. I'm not gay, ok? It was just her book that got me confused."

When Elena says nothing, I repeat "I'm *not* gay. I love Richie."

"I know you do," says Elena, looking at me straight in the eye. "Kate, you have nothing to be ashamed of. People get crushes all the time, married or not. That doesn't make you a bad person. Everyone gets attracted to other people. It's human nature. It doesn't make you a horrible wife."

Hearing her say these words makes me feel a little bit better about my inappropriate crush.

"Listen," says Elena, looking at me in the way only a best friend can. "You were wrong. She knows it and you know it. But what about what she did to you first? She clearly did not read your story, Kate. She skimmed it, pretended she read it, and then said really mean and insensitive comments about it. You saw her as someone you trusted. It was hurtful, what she did. I don't blame you for going overboard. You only did to her what she did to you."

I think about that and nod. "Maybe you're right. But I'm so scared she's actually going to call the police on me. And what if she does tell Richie? What will I do?"

I begin to cry at this awful thought.

"You need to tell Richie yourself," suggests Elena, "before he finds out from Charli. I honestly don't think she has the grounds to call the police on you, but what do I know? I can't believe she threatened you like that. What a cold-hearted bitch."

I stare down at my hands. I cringe at Charli being called that word.

"You're a good person, Kate," reminds Elena. "You and I know who you really are. Ok? Just because you fucked up doesn't mean you're a horrible person. How many times did you apologize? A hundred? Yeah. I don't even know why you feel so bad about it. She ripped your story apart and then got angry with you for standing up for yourself."

I nod resolutely. I know, deep down inside, that she is right on some level.

"I can't stand the fact that she insults me like that by basically calling me a psychopath, and she gets to have the last word," I say, shaking my head.

"Listen," says Elena firmly, "I know you want to smooth things over with this woman, but just let it go, Kate. I do think she will seriously call the police if you contact her again. Just let it go. You don't need this."

"You're right," I say determinedly. "Fuck this. Fuck this whole situation. I'm done with it, Elena."

"Good."

Chapter 9

That night, Richie and I sit on the couch eating popcorn and watching Netflix. I am so nervous that I don't even know what is on.

"Richie," I say with a sigh. "I have to tell you something."

Richie pauses to give me a curious look and stops the TV. "What, babe?"

I bite my lip, resigning myself to just say it.

"I know this is weird," I begin, playing with my fingers, "but I- well, I kind of got a little crush on Charli Diaz."

Richie gives me a blank look and rolls his eyes. "You think I didn't know that?"

I am shocked. "Huh?"

"All that reading and crying and obsessively talking about her," says Richie with a shake of his head. "I pretty much figured that out, Kate."

"And that doesn't bother you?"

Richie shrugs. "It's just a crush, who cares?"

I take a deep breath. "I sent her a hummingbird figurine, Richie. I only sent it because of her book, I promise!"

Again, Richie shrugs. "Ok. But I can kind of understand why she thinks you're psycho."

"You honestly think she should have threatened the police on me?" Now, my cheeks grow red with anger again.

Richie looks at me. "Kate, you sent a gift to her house after telling her to go fuck herself. It's kind of weird."

"I disagree," I say, crossing my arms.

Richie doesn't have a clue as to what I have been through with Charli.

"Let it go, Kate," he says, echoing Elena's words. "It doesn't matter. She doesn't want to talk to you again. This could become a legal thing. We don't have the money for that shit right now. Please just don't respond."

"Ok," I sigh. "I won't." And I mean it- at least for the moment.

I notice that Charli has deleted and blocked me off of all social media. This hurts, but I'm too angry to be sad about it.

On Monday, I cannot concentrate on work, and I am snippy with my coworkers. Not even Manny can cheer me up. I am too preoccupied with thoughts of how much Charli hates me. The former remorse I had before has also been stripped away and left a seething anger in its place. She hurt me incredibly, and she should know it.

The police? Was she fucking serious?

When I get home after the long day, I take to my computer. There is a sick feeling of dread inside of me. I have a very bad feeling that I should not be reaching out to Charli. However, in the cloud of pain and fury I am currently living in, I decide to write back anyway.

"To Charli Diaz,

"I hate that it has come to this, but I must protect myself, my family, and my own property now that you have threatened me. I am writing this letter to protect my innocence. Again, I am sending this message not to remain in any contact with you, but to prove that I want NOTHING to do with you, your family, or your property, and to sincerely ask you to NOT contact me again. This email is in response to your very serious threat, and I'm writing this as proof of my own innocence in this matter.

"If you would like to go ahead and call the police on me, feel free to do so, as this letter is not threatening in any way. I think the police should know that I never had or will have ANY intention of

hurting anyone. Not only was the threat completely ludicrous and uncalled for, but it was also extremely triggering. I was worried sick for days about what you were going to try to do to me, especially since you know where I live. You treated me like a criminal when I never did anything to harm you.

"Not to sound vain, but I know my book is good and I really don't need you to validate that for me. You ripped it to shreds and then expected me not to say anything about it. Yes, I got angry and yes, I said things I should not have said. I admitted this to you a dozen times, and I must have apologized to you at least a dozen times more, too. I understood that some of my comments were a bit harsh, considering I had taken so much of my time to read your book and you could not have cared less about mine. Yet, somehow, I turned out to be the villain here. All I did was explain why I was hurt and tell you how wonderful I thought you were. That is not a crime, Charli. You don't get to have the last word after insulting me like that.

In your book, you wrote so well about emotions and feelings that I assumed that you were a compassionate person in real life because of it. You have proven to me that this is not the case. For someone old enough to be my mother, I thought you would treat me with respect. Instead, you were bitter, spiteful, and resentful. I sincerely regret the day I saw you speak at my college and had lunch with you many years ago. I've learned nothing from you anyway.

I want to move forward with my life, and I want the same for you. I want us to go our separate ways in peace. Although you have caused me great psychological damage, I still wish the best for you because I am a kind and caring person. I wish you nothing but good things; however, I will not be threatened again without you knowing exactly where I stand.

Thanks so much for making me a stronger person!!

-With love, light, and peace,

Mrs. Kate Benson."

Satisfied with my cruel words, I smile to myself as I sit down to continue working on my book. Afterall, *she* didn't have the last word. *I* did.

Thankfully, just as I thought it would, the responses stop, and I don't hear police sirens from my window. I have succeeded in getting my point across. However, as the week drags on, the mist of rage that has been following me around like a dark cloud is beginning to dissipate. Now, it is beginning to be replaced with all of the cruel words I have said to Charli.

I go back and re-read my last message. I realize how awful it is, how dramatic I sound, and how overboard I went yet again, for the third time. Yes, Charli had hurt me. There is no denying that. She blew off my story, said very unkind things about it, and then threatened and blackmailed me. However, my response was *way* over-the-top. I realize that those are words I will never be able to take back.

The worst part is, despite all the hurt and anger dwelling inside of me, I love her. And I just irreparably hurt someone that I love. I should have just let her have the last word instead of being so disgustingly spiteful.

I throw myself onto my bed and sob dramatically for at least an hour. I cannot believe how viciously I have attacked her. I think of Charli's adorable smile and her joyful expression she always has in her pictures, and I crumble inside. I have tried to erase the light she holds so close to her- the light that makes her who she is. And by doing this, I have also destroyed my own light in the process.

A few days pass by. I take off work for two days because I cannot stop crying. I still cannot believe what happened this summer. My whole life has changed in ways I never thought it could. Before this happened, my life was so uncomplicated. There was nearly nothing going on except my boring job and writing my book. Now, it seems as if everything has shattered right in front of me.

On one of my days off, I post in my social media writer's page a cute quote I found online. Suddenly, filled with temptation, I let the arrow linger over the search bar. I know that Charli has blocked my personal page from both her personal page as well as her writing page. Suddenly, though, I wonder if she has blocked my writer's page.

To my surprise, she has not blocked my writer's page from her own writer's page.

Against my better judgement, I click on it.

She has posted some neutral things, one of her being at a restaurant and another of her dog. But then I scroll down just a bit more, and I notice she has posted something else.

"Working on this novel has been an arduous process and has not always been easy. Sometimes, I struggle to create the feelings I strive for in my writing, and sometimes I accidentally hurt other people doing so. Sometimes I wish, like it says in the song, that it was safe to just be who we are."

Underneath this, she posts *Love Song* by Lana Del Rey. I sigh as I listen to it. The lyrics are poetic and beautiful, and I can see how it is relatable to her story. I can also see, with extremely dangerous joy, that it may also relate to what she feels about me.

The lyrics ring in my head. *I'm a star and I'm burning through you…I'm a fuckin' mess, baby it's the best, now I'm here with you. I would like to think that you would stick around, you know I would die just to make you proud. I believe that you see me for who I am. Is it safe, is it safe, to be who we are?*

Although I have to really read between the lines with this one, and guess some of the meanings in her post, I just know deep down inside that this is her way of communicating with me. She has not blocked this particular page, and my heart knows her well enough to know that this may be her mysterious way of apologizing to me. It is as direct as she is able to get on a public Facebook page.

My heart soars. Perhaps she doesn't hate me after all. Perhaps she may even love me, too.

Chapter 10

Months go by. Months and months of shame and sorrow. I occasionally post deep, meaningful songs on my writer's page, hoping Charli sees them. I feel deep down that she is checking some of my social media, but I cannot be sure. I have no actual proof of this. I can only pray and hope that she sees it and is thinking of me as much as I'm thinking about her. But again, who knows?

Richie can tell something is up. I have been very distant, have tried not to talk to him about my feelings, and have even stayed late at work just to avoid being home. Elena and I go out more often and, despite having fun with my friend, I can only think about one person: Charli Diaz. She has seeped into all of my thoughts, and I am consumed by her.

I play that Lana Del Rey song over and over again, so much so that Richie has become sick of it.

"Turn that goddamn song off!" he barks one night as I cook and listen to it. "You've had that song on repeat for weeks! Can't you listen to anything else?"

I ignore him and turn it up instead. He can go fuck himself, for all I care.

My "innocent" crush has only grown through distance. I think of Charli all the time. When I'm at work, when I'm trying to relax, when I'm out with other people, or watching TV with Richie- she is all I can think about. Everything reminds me of her, and there are so many things I want to tell her, so many things I want to talk to her about. Yet, I probably will never get that opportunity again. I have irreparably ruined it all with my dramatically insane confessions.

As time moves forward, I also start seeing hummingbirds everywhere. I see them on TV, on Instagram, on Facebook, on Pinterest, on the backs of cars, on clothing, on jewelry, and I even hear people mentioning them often. People at work make references to hummingbirds, documentaries randomly pop up on Netflix about hummingbirds, and I have even seen a hummingbird land on my porch- in *October*. I have never noticed so many hummingbird references in my entire life, and they don't stop.

I find myself bursting into tears at random moments, or listening to sad music, and I know internally that I will never be the same again. No matter what ends up happening, the encounter with Charli has changed me permanently. Not only has it matured me a bit, but it has also shown me how powerful my own anger can be, and how capable I actually am of evil. To say such horrible things was not something I would ever suspect myself of, yet I said them. And I said them to someone I admire.

I try fruitlessly to manifest Charli back into my life. I watch videos about manifestation, call on the

Universe for help, and beg the heavens to bring her back to me in some way. Love songs remind me of her now, instead of Richie. I am hopelessly in love with her- all because she wrote a story in such a touching, inspiring way that I connected to her words, to her soul. Her book is not Charli, of course, but it is a deep part of her- a part that she shared with me, a part that she entrusted to me. I can't help but care for the amazing writer who wrote it.

It was an awful Christmas through and through. Richie dragged me to his mother's house where the two of them argued about politics for over an hour. Usually, I'd be fiercely engaged in this topic, but on that night, I just wanted to go home.

Now that the holiday season has finally passed, I decide that I cannot do this any longer. I cannot leave those cruel things the last thing I ever say to Charli Diaz.

I have to talk to her.

I know this is a huge risk. I know she most likely won't respond and, if she does, it could be heart-breaking. If extremely angry, she may also call the police for harassment. Either way, it's going to be a gamble. But it's been many months now and I have to do it.

I take to my computer again and type out a message, this time more serious and sincere than it was before.

"Dear Charli,

Please don't call the police- I just wanted to send my deepest regrets and apologies for what occurred over the summer. I have had time to reflect on what happened and I understand my reaction more clearly, although I did not understand it then.

When you presented me with your feedback on my own book and it was very negative, it hurt my feelings because I wanted you to love it like I loved yours. Instead of taking your advice constructively, I took it the wrong way and said many hurtful and untruthful things simply out of spite, like a little child. I think that both of our stories meant a lot to us, and I think we were hurt by each other's comments for that reason. I am sorry I reacted so terribly to your feedback. I am incredibly sorry for hurting your feelings.

I DO understand that I took the feedback too personally. I was the one that asked you for your honest opinion. I know now that you were just trying to improve my writing skills and be honest with me. Perhaps you were right- perhaps I wasn't emotionally mature enough to handle it back then. Please know that my reaction was ONLY because I cared about your opinion. I wanted to impress you, and I felt like a failure when I didn't do that.

I am so deeply sorry for anything I have done to cause you pain or worry. Please only respond if you are open to friendship- a friendship that will honor your boundaries and respect your wishes at all costs. In other words, I am willing to do whatever it takes to earn back your trust and forgiveness.

Even if you end up not responding to this, I want you to know that I will still be your biggest fan when your book comes out, and I cannot wait to see it in stores. Never stop writing. You are gold.

-Kate"

I shake as I re-read it. This is it. I'm going to send it. A part of me knows it's foolish to do this, as we both essentially made huge, very serious threats towards each other, yet a bigger part of me knows that if I don't reach out one last time, it will haunt me forever.

I can feel my hands shake again. This is an impulsive move. I hope I will not regret it. Without overthinking, like I tend to do, I take a deep breath as I hit "*send.*"

I close my eyes as if my computer is about to explode right in front of me. When I open them, I hastily close it shut and silently wait to hear sirens of police coming to arrest me for harassment.

My stomach is in my throat, and I realize that it might very well stay there for however long it takes for Charli to get back to me- which may be never. I understand then that I might have to live the rest of my life in perpetual stomach-in-throat mode.

I watch Netflix and I don't go near my phone, as I'm too afraid to see if she has or has not responded. I can sense Richie's frustration, as I am sure he's trying to call me, but I am too nervous to go anywhere near my phone.

When Richie gets back from the golf course, I am in an almost full panic. I am wondering what Charli could be thinking about my email. I pretend to be fine, although I'm crashing inside, and then I fake being tired so that I can just go upstairs to sleep. I have no interest in watching the news, which is what Richie always wants to watch. I certainly don't need any more bad news.

After I brush my teeth and do my skin care routine, I get changed into my nightgown and sit on my bed. I know that I have to look at the phone at some point. With trembling hands, I take it and tap it, watching it light up. So far, my phone has not indicated anything from Charli. I sigh in relief. I do want her to respond, of course, but at least she has not threatened me or called the police.

I silently pray that she has seen it, is thinking it over, and is planning to reach out soon.

Two weeks go by. Two weeks of complete silence. My nerves have now given way to disappointment, and I am pretty sure that I will never hear from

Charli again. Well, at least I tried, right?

It's nighttime when I am sitting and editing my novel for the hundredth time. I have my head in my hands and am feeling increasingly frustrated with the whole plot of my story. I am about to slam the laptop closed when I hear a ping go off on my phone.

Yawning, I take a look at it. There, on the screen, is an alert. It is from Charli.

I almost don't want to look at it. I've had these hopes of reconciliation for so long and any negative response will definitely crush me. I've practically begged the Universe to bring her back to me, some way, somehow. If she has responded in any kind of anger or resentment, I know I will break.

Swallowing even though my throat is completely dry, I bring up my email on the laptop where I can see it better.

"*Kate,*

"*Your email has me crying. I don't even know what to say.*

"*I'm sorry it took me this long, but I needed time to process all of this. I have a much better understanding of where you were coming from. I have given this a lot of thought. I did not mean to hurt your feelings- I was merely trying to be objective. But I see now that my comments were not simply objective, but they were also hurtful. Especially since your book really, truly is beautiful. I mean that. I am sorry I hurt you, and I am sorry I threatened you.*

"At the time, I was feeling worried because I wasn't sure what was going on with you. When we stopped talking, it took me some time, but I realized that I lost a good friend. I understand where your anger was coming from, and I'm sorry you were going through so much back then. I wish I could have been there to help you.

"Kate- I do appreciate your email. Of course, we can be friends. I am pleasantly surprised that you reached out and even have any desire at all to be connected. I'd be happy to let all of this go already. It's a new year now. Like you said, life is far too short, especially when it comes to the people who mean something to us. I'm here for you, whenever you need me. Perhaps we can laugh about this over coffee one day.

"Thank you for reaching out,

-Charli"

It is so simple. Yet, just like her writing is, so beautiful. I am in so much shock that I reread her message about twenty more times just to make sure I'm reading it correctly. I cannot believe that she has responded to me- and that I'm not in handcuffs at the same time.

I sob into my hands, realizing how lucky I have gotten. I can never mess this opportunity up- never again. I vow to myself that I will never do anything to disappoint or hurt Charli in any way ever again.

That night, I play the Lana Del Rey song that I've come to associate with Charli before I finally pass out, tears of joy running down my face in a very dramatic fashion to say the least.

My manifestations and my prayers have worked. She has come back to me. And I will not do anything to fuck it up this time.

Chapter 11

I am too elated to concentrate at work.

"Girl, what is going on in your head?" says Manny, tapping me on the shoulder. "You look like you just got laid. Richie finally figuring it out?"

I roll my eyes and laugh. "Poor Richie."

"Poor Richie? Poor you!" shouts Manny, walking around my desk. "Listen, I'm having a party at my apartment- two weeks from tomorrow. You and Richie should come- unless you want to bring someone else?"

I know he is just joking with me, but him insinuating that I would want someone else to come with me to his party makes me feel uneasy.

Manny catches on. Of course, he does. He always does.

"Girl, what's going on?" he says, leaning forward. "Tell me! Tell me!"

"Listen," I say, bending my head down, "you cannot tell anyone. I mean *any*one!"

"There's no one else here I talk to besides you and Rian anyway," says Manny, rolling his eyes. "I won't tell anyone. You're having an affair, aren't you?"

I shake my head rigorously. "No, Manny. But I do have a crush on someone. I told Richie so he already knows. He doesn't seem too bothered by it. In fact, I think he thinks it's funny."

Manny's eyes went wide, and he put his chin in his hand. "Let me guess. The lady who critiqued your book, right?"

Surprised, I nod. "Yes! How the hell did you know that?"

"I have my ways," he says mysteriously. "But didn't she threaten the fuzz on you?"

I can't help but giggle at that now. "She did. But I reached out and apologized again, and this time she actually accepted it. *And* she apologized to me. I think everything is going to be ok now."

Manny gives me a look that basically says, *Are you sure?*

I laugh. "Either way, I can pretty much bet that Richie won't come to the party. You know he hates to go anywhere. Maybe I *will* ask Charli."

Manny winked. "There ya go, girl! Ooh, my girl's about to have an affair with a *lady*!"

I shake my head and pretend to kick him from my desk.

"First, we should go out for coffee," I tell him. "Maybe if that goes well, I'll ask her to the party."

"Either way, you better be there, bitch," he says, playfully pointing his finger at me. He rolls his eyes again. "I have way too many White-girlfriends, I swear."

I laugh and turn back to the computer. I am wondering how to casually ask Charli to meet me in person. Afterall, it won't feel like we're really friends unless I can see her face, hear her voice, and give her a hug.

Hesitant but hopeful, I type a message to her.

"I'm not sure if you're busy this weekend, but did you want to grab a cup of coffee? We can talk about querying if you'd like! It might be cool."

Cool. Did I actually use that word?

I wait like an impatient child for her to see the message and write back.

"Sure!" she writes. "Saturday is my nephew's christening, and that night I'm meeting with another friend, but Sunday afternoon would be good."

"Great!" I type. "Where did you want to meet?"

"I know we live about an hour from each other, so maybe halfway?"

"I don't mind driving closer to you. I like it up there better anyway. Name your favorite coffee place."

"In that case, let's go to The Brew," she says, referring to a somewhat well-known café in her area. "They have the best brownies, too!"

I smile. This is beyond my wildest hopes. I have gotten my one wish, my one prayer that I have been begging the Universe for all of this time. My dream has come true- Charli has forgiven me, we are friends, and we are going to meet up in person.

I am elated when I arrive home. Richie is back from work early and wants to go out to eat. I excitedly agree. Mainly because I want to get out of the house, but also because I am in a celebratory mood.

When we get to the restaurant and sit down, Richie looks at me suspiciously.

"You seem happy today," he says. "Is it because that woman is talking to you again? You know, your little lesbo crush?"

I am tempted to complain but instead I just say, "Yep!"

He rolls his eyes and digs into his sandwich. I play around with my spaghetti, twirling the noodles around and around with my fork.

"So how was work?" I ask him, trying to think of something to talk about. Recently, it is always so hard to talk to Richie about anything.

He just shrugs and continues to eat, hardly pausing and not glancing up. This frustrates me. Afterall, I'm trying to have a conversation here!

"I've missed going out to eat," I say, attempting again. "This is really nice."

Richie nods, a piece of ham falling out of his mouth. Sometimes I really cannot stand him.

I roll my eyes and glance at my phone. I notice that Charli has "loved" one of my pictures on Facebook. This makes me smile.

"What's so great?" asks Richie, his mouth full.

I sigh. "Nothing, Richie. Just eat your sandwich.

I cannot help but wish I was with Charli instead. Men. Men are so gross sometimes.

That Sunday afternoon, I am stressed out. Richie is sitting and watching the news again as I get ready for my meet-up with Charli.

"Wow, you look really hot," he says, giving me a suspicious look. "What's with the boob top and heels? And all that eyeshadow? You look like you just came back from a strip club."

I shrug and laugh it off. "Nothing, Richie. This is how I look when I go out with my friends."

"Not the last time I've seen," he mutters as he turns the news up.

I sigh and grab my purse. I make sure I have an ample supply of mints just in case, and a little mirror to check on my makeup throughout the day. I don't say goodbye to Richie. He won't hear me over the TV anyway.

I step into my car and give myself a quick look in the mirror. I really do look very pretty. Maybe it is too much. Maybe it will be too obvious.

This thought makes me feel a bit worried, so I smudge my red lipstick so it's just a little bit lighter. It's the first time I'm seeing Charli in thirteen years, and I really don't want to creep her out again. I did a fine job already last time.

Coincidentally, that Lana Del Rey song comes on my Spotify. I take it as a good sign, although the closer I get to The Brew, the more nervous I am growing. By the time I am in the parking lot- twenty minutes early, by the way- I am shaking from head to toe. I suddenly don't think I can do this.

I momentarily consider texting Charli that I got into a fender-bender and can't come, but I shrug that idea off. If I don't see her now, I never will.

I pop a mint into my mouth, finish listening to a song that makes me laugh, and then hesitantly walk into the café. Of course, me being so early, Charli is not there.

I take a seat on the right side by one of the windows. I am so nervous that I can hardly remember my name. I have no idea how this is going to go. For months and months, all I could think about was Charli Diaz and how important she is to me. Now, the dream is realized, and we are finally meeting face-to-face. What if she thinks I'm unattractive? What if the mints I ate don't work? What if I get so nervous that I cannot speak, just like that time all those years ago in my college's dining hall? What if she ends up hating our time together?

It feels like forever as I sit there and tremble in my seat. I have got to get my nerves together. She cannot know the fear I am experiencing. That would be humiliating.

Damn, why didn't I ask her to a bar instead? At least some drinks would loosen me up.

I stand up, attempting to shake off my nerves, and then I see her.

Of course, she's aged a bit since the last time I saw her in person. However, she has not aged nearly as much as most people do, and she is just as beautiful as always. Her hair, a shade of darker blonde than before, now stops at her shoulders, and she has just very slightly more folds above her cheeks. Other than that, she hardly looks any different than she did when she was in her forties. She still has that youthful glow about her, and I am once again mesmerized.

She doesn't recognize me at first. She glances at me for a moment before moving around her eyes. Have I really changed that much?

I slowly and carefully walk over to her. I am nervous, but I try to smile as confidently as I possibly can. As I get closer, she turns towards me. For a second, she looks surprised. Then, she immediately begins walking over to me, that bright smile on her face.

As I walk closer, I say, "Is it ok to hug you?"

Charli nods. "Of course, it is, Kate!"

I step towards her and envelope her in an awkward, slightly stiff hug. I do not want to creep her out or chase her away by being over-the-top. However, she hugs me with more of a force until I am obliged to hold her more tightly.

Out of nowhere, my eyes fill with tears. I cannot believe this woman is standing in front of me after all of this time and all of this heart-ache.

"Kate! Oh Kate!" she begins frantically.

"I am so sorry," I choke. "I'm so sorry for everything." And then the tears come rolling down my face, one after another, in an embarrassment of succession.

"Let's sit down," she says, and we walk to the table where I have kept my purse at.

"Don't cry," she says sternly but warmly. "It's all over now. It's in the past. Remember? It's a new year."

I sniffle and try to force myself to stop crying before I begin to hyperventilate. I realize then how much I have truly missed her.

"I'm sorry," I manage to repeat. "I didn't think I was going to cry."

"Don't be," she says, her eyes sparkling. "It's fine. Get it together so I can hear all about your life."

I laugh through my tears and am finally able to speak like a normal person.

"My life isn't very interesting," I say, wringing my hands anxiously in my lap. Charli is still intimidatingly beautiful. "As you know, I've been married a while now. Richie is a nice guy. He gets on my nerves, but he's a nice guy."

"Men," she says with a laugh.

I nod awkwardly as the waitress comes to take our orders.

"That book of yours was really a success," she says. "I'm so proud of you."

I glow. She said she is *proud* of me.

"What about yours?" I say. "*The Ruby Cove* is fantastic. I haven't met one person who read it that didn't love it."

She slightly blushes, which catches me off guard for some reason.

"It's not always the easiest task in the world to write, as you know," she says. "All we can do is try our best. I should tell you now that I am also sorry for what I said before. I truly did love your book, Kate. I really did."

"No," I shake my head. "You don't have to say that. Really."

"I mean that," she says softly. "Your story was beautiful, and the world-building was fantastic. I'm sorry I didn't indicate that to you in the first place."

"Please, never be sorry again," I say, surprising myself by how firm I sound. "Remember, it's in the past now."

"In the past," she says cheerfully.

We then get into a conversation about querying literary agents and how much of a pain in the ass it is. Charli has already sent some queries out and is waiting on replies. I explain to her that I am also about to begin the process.

"It's hard to put yourself out there," she says. "Sometimes, we have to get rejections to get to the agent that is right for us."

"True," I say with a smile.

For a moment we just stare at each other. I feel my cheeks getting red, and I am so hypnotized by her sapphire eyes that I forget to look away.

"I know you'll find the right agent for you," she assures me. "Just don't give up. Keep doing the work and good things will come your way."

Just being in Charli's presence is awe-inspiring. Her gentle voice, her vivid soul that shines right through her eyes, her sincere, warm smile- it all has me hypnotized.

"I've missed you," I say suddenly. I surprise myself, as I did not expect to be so bold. "I bet that doesn't make a lot of sense."

She gives me a sad look and says, "It does make sense. It makes a lot of sense. I've missed you, too.

I am elated. She has missed me, too.

"This is nice," she says, looking directly into my eyes.

I nod, still feeling self-conscious but a bit less so now that we're talking. In fact, the meeting seems to be so much shorter than I thought it would be, and two hours goes by fast.

"I do have to get going," she says, looking at her phone. "But it's been so nice to see you, Kate."

"You too," the disappointment in my voice is obvious. "Thanks for coming."

"No, thank *you*," she answers. "I know this was far for you. Next time, we'll meet closer to you."

Next time? So, she wants to meet up again! My heart flies.

"I know a great restaurant we can go to," I say without thinking. I am surprised by how brave I feel in this moment. "Let's make plans to go soon. Maybe in a couple of weeks?"

The truth is that I want to see Charli the very next day, but I can't say that of course.

Charli looks pleasantly surprised and gives me sort of a half-grin.

"Let's do it."

We agree to reconnect and then we both walk outside and back to our cars. Before I get inside of mine, she says, "Kate?"

"Yeah?"

She looks like she wants to say something important but, instead, she says, "So good to see you. Bye!"

I wave and step into my car. This meet-up could not have gone better. Yes, I was shy and nervous, and I did cry like a fool, but Charli made me feel comfortable even through the awkwardness of our past. She made me feel like that ugly spot in our relationship didn't matter at all- that it was truly a thing of the past and just a strange misunderstanding. It was like we had entered a whole new chapter entirely and were truly getting to know each other the way the Universe had always intended.

"How was your date?" Richie says sarcastically when I arrive home.

"My *meeting* with my friend was fine," I say in frustration. "I'm going to go do some work on my query letter."

"Ok, I guess we'll watch TV later?"

"I guess," I say, walking up the stairs before he can say anything else.

When I get to my office, I am swept up in a wave of happiness. Everything had been so terrible for so long, and now things are finally good again- actually, better than before. I have Charli back in my life, and this time we are *actual* friends. This time, I am not going to fuck this up.

I look at myself in the mirror, satisfied that I do look pretty good. Maybe Charli thinks I am just as pretty as I think she is. That is the hope, at least.

I cannot wait until we go to the restaurant. I want to text her immediately but, realizing how desperate that may look, I hold off. Instead, I let myself enjoy the recent memory of the two of us sipping coffee at the café, talking about books and inspiration. It had been such a pleasant time. I never wanted the meeting to end. I could have spent hours and hours with her. Yet, I would have to wait a couple of weeks. That was the deal.

Chapter 12

I pretend to be cool for a while. I do not text or message Charli the next day or even the day after that. This time, I am hoping that she will be the one to reach out first.

This time, she is.

"Hey Kate!" she texts me on the third day. "Are you free anytime soon?"

I smile. "Yes! I was going to ask you if you still wanted to go to that restaurant I was telling you about. It's called Quaker's. They have really good bread."

I shake my head at how stupid my text message sounds. Good *bread*? Really?

She puts a smiley emoji next to her text that reads, "Sounds good! When works for you?"

The truth is that I have no weekend plans coming up for the rest of my life besides Manny's party at his place. So, anytime would be good.

"What about this weekend?" I write, hoping it doesn't sound too soon.

Along with another smiley emoji, she answers, "Sounds good! Saturday night?"

"Sure! 6pm?"

"Perfect."

And so, it is. Another outing with Charli, the pinnacle of my desires. I know Richie is going to be suspicious, but I no longer care. In fact, the thought of spending every single weekend for the rest of my life with this man is almost unbearable. He can suck it.

As expected, I get to Quaker's way earlier than Charli does. As I wait, I nervously reapply my lipstick in the car. This time, I am dressed up quite fancy in a little black dress with accented gold jewelry. Quaker's is a pretty nice restaurant, and I didn't choose it for no reason. Charli should know that I have good taste.

I walk in and tell the host about my reservation. Yes, it's *that* kind of restaurant. I silently hope this doesn't bring up any red flags for Charli.

The host leads me to a candle-lit table towards the back, where there are fewer tables surrounding us. For a second, I almost protest. It looks a little bit *too* private, and I don't want Charli to freak out. Afterall, she knows that I have had feelings for her in the past. What she may or may not know is that my feelings have only grown since the last time saw her.

I hesitate but then nod. It can't be that bad.

After I sit and twiddle my thumbs for fifteen minutes, I see Charli walk through the door, bringing all the light she carries with her right inside.

I can't help but stare at her as she approaches me. Charli is a natural beauty, so I'm not surprised she looks good, but- wow. She is dressed in a black dress with swirly patterns that reach just above her knees, high black heels, and diamond earrings. Her lips are a bright red that makes her hair look blonder, and she has on smoky gray eye shadow. Her smile is youthful and lights up her whole face.

The host gives her a menu as she sits down, and we order a bottle of wine.

I cannot take my eyes off of her. Like the character, Melanie, described in her book, Charli is like the sun- dangerous to look at, but more beautiful and brighter than anything you can see. I quickly think about Charli's book and how Violet felt that exact way about Melanie.

I can tell she knows I'm staring at her because she gives me a sheepish smile. Trying to shake myself out of it, I say, "It's great to see you again! Thanks for driving out here!"

"I didn't mind at all," she answers. "It's pretty around here. How long have you lived in this town?"

"Richie and I moved here about five years ago now," I answer. "It's not too bad. I like that there's some good restaurants near us."

"That always helps," she says.

Her voice is, as usual, smooth as butter, and I want to listen to every word she says. Unlike it was at the café, what I *really* want to do is to connect. Not just talk about agents and literature and queries, but actually get to *know* her. I'm going to have to be braver this time.

"Charli," I begin, clearing my throat, "what is your favorite book of all time?"

She looks surprised by how deep of a question I give her right off the bat. But I don't want to make cheerful chatter. I want to know her heart.

"I don't have one," she says with a shrug. "I love too many, for all different reasons! I couldn't pick just one."

"I don't think I can either," I agree, the waitress bringing us our wine. I take a big sip of it, hoping it will help calm my nerves.

She smiles at me, and I try not to make it obvious that I'm swooning over her.

We sip our wine quietly for a minute. I am worried that the pause is too long, and she will get easily bored of me.

Without thinking, I say, "You look really pretty."

I can't believe I just said that. What the hell is wrong with me?

But Charli doesn't seem disturbed. Her eyes sparkle at me and her skin glows from the candlelight, as well as her natural fire she carries within her body. "So do you, Kate."

Such an innocent compliment. Just a nice gesture because I had complimented her first. Yet, this makes my heart beat fast.

"How is your family?" I say, attempting politeness.

"They're all fine," she answers. "Well, for the most part."

I wonder what she means.

"The most part?" I ask.

She clears her throat and sighs. "My husband and I recently separated. He's moved out now. Since my daughter lives in Denver, I feel pretty alone sometimes."

This statement shocks me. I always had this idea that Charli has this perfect life and perfect relationship with her husband. At least, that's what it looks like on Facebook. Yet, I remind myself, social media is usually nothing like real life. We are just merely masks on the internet, just pretending.

"I'm so sorry to hear that," I say, feeling genuinely sad. The thought of Charli going through such turmoil hurts my heart.

"It's really not that bad," she says with a shrug. "Yes, sometimes I get a bit lonely. I miss my daughter especially. But now I can have my friends over anytime I want! It's pretty great."

I smile and narrow my eyes. It's a habit I do when I have a crush someone- I smile and narrow my eyes. I hope Charli can't see through me.

"Sometimes, things just don't work out," she says to me with a sigh. "My ex-husband and I are still friends. We get along outside the marriage, but we just couldn't compromise within it, if that makes sense."

It makes a *lot* of sense to me, and I nod.

"I don't think I could get along with Richie either way," I mutter before thinking.

Charli looks up from her wine, surprised.

"You and Richie don't get along?"

I shake my head. "We used to. We don't anymore. I don't know why, but we annoy the hell out of each other now. I think we're growing apart. I hate to believe it, but I'm pretty sure that's what's happening. We don't agree on anything, and he hardly includes me in anything in his life, so I stopped including him in mine."

Charli looks concerned. To lighten the mood, I add, "Great wine!"

But Charli doesn't let it go right away.

"Have you tried couples counseling?" she asks.

I nod. "Actually, we have. Last year. It didn't do anything but make us angrier with each other."

Charli nods. "I know that feeling. That's why sometimes it's best to let things go before they completely wither away."

I ponder what she says. She has a good point.

We soon take our dinner orders and I ask for more wine. I still cannot stop staring at her. She is just a ball of energy herself, a breath of fresh air. I cannot believe I'm actually sitting in front of her. This time, though, I'm not a little college kid looking up to her like a puppy. This time, I'm a grown woman- a woman who has fallen helplessly in love with her and has no idea what to do about it.

"Well, have you dated anyone since the separation?" I try to ask this casually, but it comes out forced.

She sighs. "I've been on a date here and there. It's been ok. I haven't really found a man I'm very interested in."

My heart drops when she says, "a man." Perhaps she would never even consider dating a woman, and her story was just that- a story. Maybe she wasn't even attracted to women at all.

I try to shake off this discouraging thought, but it bothers me. I know that it *shouldn't* bother me. Yet, isn't it always the things that shouldn't get to us that get to us the most?

I then dare to ask the question. The question I've been wanting to ask her since she sent me her story last summer.

"Where did you find the inspiration to write that beautiful love story?" I ask, looking at her carefully.

Her eyes widen and, for a second, I regret asking. But then she relaxes and says, "It just kind of came to me. I wanted to write a story about someone saving someone else's life, and the other person continuing to live on even after they were gone."

It's a beautiful thing to say, but it's even more beautiful coming from her voice.

"It was- well, it was magic," I say, feeling my cheeks heat up again.

When I look into her eyes, I can sense what she is feeling. As crazy as it sounds, even to me, I somewhat believe me and this woman have some weird kind of telepathic connection. I feel that our souls recognize each other. I wonder if she ever feels that way, too.

The wine helping me feel more and more bold with every sip, I say shamelessly, "Were Violet and Melanie real people?"

The corners of her mouth lift up very subtly. "In a sense, I'd say. I sort of completely made up Violet, as I wanted a protagonist readers would root for. But Melanie? Yes, she was real."

My curiosity is at its peak now, and completely overcomes any timidness I am feeling.

"She must have been very special, the way you write about her," I can't help but notice the tinge of jealousy in my own voice.

Charli smiles but looks down into her wine glass. That is when I know to drop the subject.

"I also really like that you included the Jersey Shore in your book," I say quickly, hoping I didn't push too hard. "It was cool reading about some of the places."

She laughs. "There's no place like home, as they say."

When she looks over at me, I feel a shock of electricity run through my whole body. I suddenly find myself staring again. I quickly divert my gaze, but I'm pretty sure she has just seen right through me.

She knows that I still have feelings for her. In fact, she may even know that I have fallen completely in love with her.

When I glance up, she is looking at me, too, in a completely calm and controlled way. I keep her gaze for a moment before saying, "Isn't this a nice place?"

Charli nods. "It's lovely, Kate."

I smile and pretend to eat my salad, but I am becoming nervous again. I sip more wine and stare into my hands. Suddenly, I have no idea what to talk about.

In that easy, carefree way that she did back all of those years ago at my college dining hall, she starts up the conversation again, almost as if there was never a lull to begin with. I wonder how she does this so well.

"What about you? What inspired your own book?"

I remember my graphic sex scenes and outwardly cringe. I know she has seen this so I simply shrug. "I have no idea. That stupid plot just came to me. Too many romcoms, I guess."

"Well, I love a good romcom!" she says cheerfully. When she smiles, the entire room around me lights up. It's as if she has some kind of superpower that makes everything around her just glisten.

After a full moment, I realize I have just been staring into her eyes and grinning at her. I look quickly at the wall next to me.

She continues on like nothing happened and I'm not a complete weirdo.

"It's been nice taking a break from writing," she says casually. "I've had more time to do other things- you know, like shop and stuff." She chuckles and it makes me smile.

"I see so many pictures of your dog on Facebook," I say. "He's so cute! Or she?"

"Yes, he is sometimes," she answers, "especially when he's not destroying my shoes."

I smile. "I used to have a dog. Just like you wrote about in your story, losing a dog is one of the worst things you can go through in life."

"I've had so many dogs," she says, "and it doesn't get easier!"

"I can imagine," I say, starting to feel more comfortable again. "When did you know you wanted to be a writer?"

She shrugs. "I guess it started when I learned how to write. I used to love hearing my grandmother's stories, and it made me want to tell my own. What about you, Kate?"

"I can't remember a time when I didn't want to be a writer," I say, now actually realizing this for the first time. "I think I wanted to be a writer before I could even write."

"It's in your blood," she says, taking another sip of wine.

I have a strange, fleeting thought of wishing it was me that her lips were touching instead of the rim of the glass.

Admonishing myself for this thought, I ask the waiter for more wine.

Charli and I sit and chat for a long time. She talks about her daughter, how proud she is of her, and how happy she is with the way she grew up. She doesn't provide too many details, but she does say that she and her husband had split for irreconcilable differences, and overall, just wanted to experience life on their own terms. I give her some insight into my own crumbling marriage and find out we have more in common that I even thought we did.

I vacillate between extreme shyness and total comfort. Being around someone so magnetic is intimidating, but Charli makes it easy to be around her. There is nothing pretentious or snobbish about her, despite her beauty and success. She is as real as the earth under my feet but at the same time as difficult to define as the stars in the sky.

"What inspired you to talk about hummingbirds?" I ask her, leaning on my elbow, trying to make my eyes shine like hers do.

She smiles. "A good friend used to love them," she said. "And, oddly enough, they seemed to love her back. Sometimes I'd go visit, and there would be hummingbirds randomly sitting on her porch. It was the strangest thing. When she passed away, I put a hummingbird figurine in her coffin."

"Just like Violet did with Melanie," I reflect, the wine making me feel warm.

"To answer your question about Melanie better," she says, "yes, I did know someone once that inspired Melanie. She was my best friend in college, and we did everything together. You could never meet someone as courageous as Sharon. When she got cancer, it just sucked the life out of all of us. She knew she was going to die young, and she had always said it, long before she was even diagnosed. She did die very young, at only twenty-five." Here, she clears her throat and her eyes begin to appear glassy.

"I'm so sorry," I peep, for there is truly nothing else I can say. "I honestly can't imagine that."

She nods sadly. "You were right about what you said. It *is* important to tell the people around you how you feel about them. Because you never know when it will be the last time."

We finish up dinner and head outside into the cold air. We walk to our cars, which happen to be coincidentally parked right next to each other, and I pause.

"Hey, Charli," I say, twirling my keys in my hand. "Let's do this again soon?"

She nods and her whole face lights up. "Sounds good, Kate. I would love that."

And I can tell by her expression that she genuinely means it.

When I finally get home, I'm in a great mood- so great that I even sit with Richie and watch the news. We talk and laugh like old times, and I momentarily forget that I am not in love with him.

The thought of not being in love with Richie hurts. I did not get married to eventually get a divorce. But I would be lying if I said I didn't think about it often.

"How was your hot date with the writer lady?" he asks me as we get changed into night clothes.

I try to act casually, but the joy on my face is obvious. "It was fine."

"Seems more than fine to me," he says suspiciously, his eyes narrowing. "You were dressed to the nines tonight! At first, I thought you were going to a nightclub in New York."

I ignore his comment and brush out my hair.

"Maybe you should think about spending some time with me instead of going on dates with your girlfriend," he says to me suddenly.

I turn around sharply. "What the hell does that mean?"

"What do you think it means, Kate?" he asks with a sigh. "You are obsessed with this woman. You think I haven't noticed?"

I bite my lip. He's not wrong.

"Listen, I'm sorry," I say, feeling guilt bubble up to the surface. "I just admire her, that's all. Maybe this weekend we can spend some time together? Maybe we can do something other than watch the news?"

At that comment, Richie's arms fly up in the air.

"Seriously?" he says in an accusatory tone. "I don't always watch the news, Kate. When I do watch it, it's because it's important to see what's going on and not be fucking stupid about the world around us."

I feel anger instead of guilt bubbling up.

"Do you have to curse at me like that?"

"You do it all the time!" he yells. "And I wasn't cursing *at* you, I was just cursing in general."

I stomp my foot like a frustrated child and throw the hairbrush on the ground.

"You know what, Richie, I tried to do something with you this weekend but, of course, you had to go ruin it. You ruin everything!"

Richie purses his lips and shakes his head. I know that look very well. That's his, *You've gone too far* look.

"Ok, not *every*thing-"

"If that's true, then I'll stay away from you," he says through gritted teeth. "Since I apparently ruin everything, let's just stay away from each other until you figure out what it is you actually want. Because I'm pretty damn sure it's not me anymore."

With that, he leaves the bedroom in a cloud of anger.

I feel the guilt rising again like vomit, but I push it down. Afterall, it was Richie who started all of this. It was Richie who distanced himself from me first by his ridiculous thoughts of wanting to be Tim McGraw and his obsession with the damn TV. He's the one I had to beg for attention from. Now that it's me, it's suddenly a problem for him?

Nevertheless, I am overwhelmed with guilt. Here I am, a married woman, trying to impress someone else and practically going on dates. Richie never signed up for this when we got married. He never would have agreed to any of this had he known earlier.

I am quite aware that I am becoming a terrible person if I continue down this path. I am in love with someone else and am hoping this person has feelings for me, too. I am not exactly being faithful. Yet, I can't help it.

I love Richie very much, and I do want to do right by him, but everything is crumbling around me and I have no idea what to do.

I shake my head and sit on the bed, slowly petting Lila who is crawling all over me. She knows something is up.

"I'm not straight, Lila," I whisper. "I'm not sure if I'm even bi."

Chapter 13

I end up going to Manny's party alone. I thought it would be too weird to ask Charli to come with me, at least this soon, and Richie won't do anything he doesn't want to do. The party would have been good had Charli and her positive energy been filling the apartment. I couldn't help but think about her the entire time, and wishing she was there.

Soon enough, it's Valentine's Day. Instead of going on a date with my husband, I decide to meet up with Elena for dinner. Richie and I haven't talked the whole entire week, and I don't even bother asking him what he wants to do tonight.

"You're kidding me, right?" asks Elena as she stuffs a piece of garlic bread in her mouth.

I sigh. "I don't know, Elena. I just don't think I can keep up this charade anymore. Like, all we do is fight. We don't even have sex anymore and, honestly, I don't want to. I- I'm not sure if I ever even enjoyed sex with Richie."

"What!?" Elena puts down her garlic bread. "You guys have been together forever! You've *never* enjoyed having sex with him?"

"It was alright in the beginning," I reply. "I just- I don't know. Elena, the more I think about it, the more I realize that I don't think I'm straight or even bi. I think I'm a lesbian." Elena's brown eyes grow wide. "Ok, listen Kate, I know you have that crush on that lady, but you and Richie have been together for over ten years. You guys have something special."

"We *used* to," I argue, surprising myself by my fierce tone. "I love Richie so much, and I know he loves me, too. But I don't love him in *that* way. I'm not sure I ever really loved him as anything more than a friend. I *thought* I did, but then I got to know Charli, and…and it changed how I look at everything. I thought it was love with Richie, but the way I feel for him is nothing compared to the way I've been feeling for Charli. I know, I know how bad this is. You don't have to look at me like that."

Elena changes her facial expression from a motherly disappointment into a frustrated friend. "I just don't want to see you ruin your life over a little crush, Kate."

I shrug. "My life is being ruined by my own misery. I don't want to play games anymore. I just want to be myself."

"You seriously feel like you're gay?" she asks, now a look of concern crossing her face.

I sigh and nod. "I think it's always been something inside of me. It's always made me different from other people. I never thought about it because I never believed it could be true." I am shocked when I burst into tears.

Elena gets up from the table and comes to lean over and hug me.

"Shit, Kate," she says gently. "I didn't realize how serious this was. I'm so sorry. I was worried that you were rushing things. Kate, if you're a lesbian, that's totally fine! It's ok! We're gonna figure everything out, ok?"

I sniffle into the napkin and begin to laugh. "How pathetic."

Elena goes to sit back down. "Don't worry about it. But now that you know for sure, this is a conversation you're going to have to have with Richie. Divorces are so messy. Maybe you guys can just separate for a while until you figure everything out?"

"I wonder which one of us will keep the house," I say softly. "It's *our* house. The house we started together. I never thought I'd be in this position."

Elena gives me a look full of sympathy. "This is why I never got married to Jake. I knew I loved him, but I knew monogamy wasn't for either of us. I knew we'd change our minds, and who wants to go through a divorce? But take things one step at a time. You need to tell Richie the truth and then go from there. Maybe you guys will just separate, like I said."

I nod resolutely. "He deserves the truth, at least. He's a shitty husband, but he deserves the truth. He loves me, I do know that."

Elena sighs. "What are you going to do about Charli? Are you going to tell her how you feel?"

"Well, I'm pretty sure she knows that my old feelings haven't completely gone away," I say. "I think she has some inkling. I don't want to put her in the position to feel uncomfortable again and chase her away. That's the last thing I want. For now, I'm leaving it alone. I just want to see where this goes."

"True," Elena agrees, sipping her peppermint tea. "There's no reason to rush. Hey, maybe she'll be the one to tell you that she has feelings first!"

"That's if she even does," I sigh.

"Don't be so negative," chides my friend. "You never manifest anything you want by being negative. Remember, Kate, *live in the end result. Everyone is you pushed out*. That's what Neville Goddard said, anyway."

I laugh. "Well, Neville Goddard never met Charli Diaz. But I need to tell Richie first. That's going to be the hardest part."

When I get home, Richie is asleep on the couch. I almost just go to bed when he suddenly wakes up.

"Kate," he says groggily. "I got you something."

My stomach drops. I look over at the table and see that he has gotten me roses and chocolate for Valentine's Day. At this sweet gesture, I am overwhelmed with guilt and shame.

"Why are you crying?" he asks. "What's wrong?"

I shake my head. "Thank you for the gifts."

Richie comes to try to hug me, but I recoil away.

"I have to tell you something," I say, my voice shaking.

The look on his face says it all. He already knows.

"I was hoping I would have a little more time with you," he says, looking at the ground. "But I'm not stupid. I know what's going on."

"Nothing happened, Richie. Nothing. I do love you so much-" I begin.

He puts his finger up and shakes his head. "Don't do this, Kate. I don't want to hear this right now."

"But I do love you!" I cry out as he begins to walk away. "Don't leave! We have to talk!"

"Listen," he says sharply. "It's almost midnight. We are not talking about this tonight. Tomorrow, I'm hanging out with Billy in the afternoon. When I come home, we'll discuss this."

"But just talk for a minute- I'm so sorry, Richie!"

I watch him turn the corner. I feel absolutely terrible, as if I have done something horrible to someone. Perhaps, in a way, I have.

I sit on the couch and open my laptop. I need some kind of distraction. I see that Charli has sent me a message.

"Hey Kate! There's this art show at the beach next weekend. I thought you might want to come along. There should be some really amazing art!"

"I definitely need the distraction," I write. "I'll be happy to go!"

"Is everything ok?"

"Yeah," I answer. "Just the usual. I'm looking forward to seeing you."

"Likewise!" she says.

I sigh. I never wanted to hurt Richie. I love Richie. I just don't love him in *that* way. This isn't his fault though, and when I think about how I have hurt him I begin to sob into my hands. I cannot believe this is all happening. What kind of person am I? Who realizes they are not in love with their spouse and, instead, are in love with someone else? Even worse is the fact that a part of me tried to pursue these feelings while still being married. My life is completely falling apart. All because of a book.

The next day, Richie and I are sitting on the couch in the family room, staring into our hands. I am already beginning to cry, more from shame than anything else, and my tears are falling onto Lila's fur.

"How can you do this to me? To us? After everything we've been through together?" Richie chokes, his voice trembling.

"It isn't like that," I say, trying to make him understand. "This isn't easy for me. None of this is.

"It seemed pretty easy for you to go on dates with Charli and ignore me," he says.

The pain in his voice and on his face is so utterly clear. For a second, I want to run up to him and kiss him better and tell him this was all a joke. But I don't.

"I love you, I do, Richie," I say calmly. "I didn't mean to waste some of the best years of your life, ok? I…I do love you… it's just in a different way than I thought it was when we got married."

"I can't believe this," he gives a sarcastic laugh. "You weren't even in love with me when we got married?"

I realize what I have said but it's too late now.

"I swear to love you forever," I manage to say. "But I can't be with you. Not any longer. You deserve the real thing, Richie. I want you to find it."

Richie, looking so destroyed, glances at me and says, "I'm glad you found the real thing, Kate. I'm just sorry it wasn't me." And then he stands up, leaving me to sob uncontrollably into my hands.

We decide that day that it is really over. I try to make him understand that it isn't his fault, that he's the most wonderful guy I've met, and that I do truly care about him. However, I might as well have been speaking to a wall because he was just too hurt to process this information.

We are still financially dependent on each other, so we agree to stay living together for the time being, before we can figure something out. Richie states that he will look for apartments soon because I'm the one who paid more for the house anyway when I used the money I got from publishing my book. I argue with him that he should keep it, since I'm the one that is essentially breaking up the marriage, but Richie is stubborn and reminds me that I love the house and should be the one to have it. We also agree that Lila will live with me; however, Richie will come to visit Lila every other week. Thankfully, it will no longer be too awkward, as Richie decided to stay with one of his friends for a while and will be leaving in a couple of days.

The day of the art show, I know Richie knows who I am going to be with.

I wear a somewhat indie-looking hippie dress that comes to my ankles, trying to look artistic. I smear gloss on my lips and gold eye shadow on my eyes before I walk downstairs with my purse.

Richie looks over at me from the couch and shakes his head.

"Have a good time with Charli," he says sarcastically.

I sigh and don't respond. Instead, I leave the house, keys in hand, and walk to my car.

I listen to Lana Del Rey the whole way there, as her music reminds me of Charli now, and when I get to the beach, I am in a happier mood.

Afterall, I no longer have to hide who I am or who I love. I can just be me now, Kate. Kate who is still very confused about her life, but absolutely certain of whom she truly loves.

It is February and light snow has created a blanket on the sand that is quite Narnia-like. I see the artists have set up many tables, and there is already quite a crowd. I get out my phone, feeling a bit nervous, and text Charli that I am there.

"I'm here," she writes. "I'm in the middle of the exhibits. Come out and I'll find you!"

I am easy to find, being tall and red-haired, and she soon comes up beside me.

"Hey, you!" she says cheerfully.

I can't help but feel my whole face light up. "Hi! Thanks so much for inviting me."

Charli smiles in that adorable way she always does, and we begin to look at the artwork.

Charli tells me that she loves Italian art, and fell in love with it when she went to an art museum in Italy. I tell her that I am fond of most art, although some Picasso-like modern art is not my thing. Charli agrees with me, and we stroll along, our boots crunching in the snow.

"Look at this," Charli says, stopping me.

I turn to see a beautiful painting of a hummingbird. It has the most colorful plumes, and the painter created the eyes to be so life-like that I feel it is staring into my soul. In the background, there is a garden of trees and flowers of golden colors with splashes of pink. It is really a spectacular painting to behold.

"A hummingbird," I muse. I turn to Charli. "I'd like to buy this for you."

Charli immediately laughs and shakes her head. "No, no, it's fine, Kate."

Ignoring her, I ask the artist how much the price is. When he says $300, I don't bat an eye as I hand him my credit card.

"Kate, it's too expensive!" Charli is saying behind me. "Don't get it!"

"Too late," I say when the artist hands me back the card. "Can we pick the painting up later? When we're done walking around?" I ask him.

"Absolutely," says the artist with a smile.

Charli stares at me as I begin to walk.

"I don't know how people paint like that," I sigh. "I can't even draw a tree."

Charli puts her hand on my arm for a quick moment. That mere touch leaves me breathless.

"You shouldn't have bought that for me, Kate," she says. "That was way too much money."

"Don't you like it?" I ask, hoping I didn't offend her.

She smiles. "I love it. Now, when you find something you love, tell me and I will get it for you."

I turn around and look at her. "Charli, I didn't buy the painting so that you could get me something. I have too many paintings all over my house; I don't need more. I bought it because I knew you'd love it, and it's a hummingbird so it has special meaning for us. Doesn't it?"

Charli frowns and sighs. Then she smiles slightly. "It does."

"Just buy dinner next time," I say. "We'll call it even.

"Hardly," but she drops the subject then.

As we stroll along, I just want to tell her the truth. I want to tell her that I think she's brilliant, and kind, and beautiful. I want to tell her that she has lit up my life like no one ever has before and has created a fire deep within me that only keeps growing with time. Instead, I look over and say without thinking, "My husband and I split up."

Charli stops in her tracks. "Oh Kate! I am so sorry!"

I shake my head. "Don't be sorry. It's hard, but it's for the best. Richie and I had been growing distant for a long time."

"Separations are never easy," says Charli sympathetically. "I know firsthand. They are grueling and they take so much energy out of you. Is there anything I can do to help you?"

Yes. Grab my neck and put your lips on mine.

"No," I say. "Just being my friend is helpful."

She nods. "What will you do with the house?"

I sigh. "Right now, Richie is staying with his friend. It shouldn't be too long, though. He wants me to keep the house."

"Good," says Charli. "That's what my ex did, too."

I want so badly to take her hand in mind but I resist. Afterall, who am I to be so bold?

We continue to stroll around, taking in all of the talent that is here at this exhibit. As I look behind me and see the waves crashing, it suddenly reminds me of her story.

"You're so good at romance," I say. Then, I add quickly, "I mean books! You write about romance really well."

Charli's face lights up. "It's something I'm not too bad at. You're not shabby at it, yourself!"

I blush when I remember my cringey sex scenes in my book. I am hoping that she has forgotten about them.

"Romance is the most interesting to me," I say. "Everything else is great, but I feel that love is really the purpose of life. You know, to love and be loved. Everything else seems secondary in comparison."

She turns her head to the side. "You know what, that's so true, Kate. Love gives everything else meaning! Even the bad times."

I nod in agreement, hoping that I planted a seed that would blossom into loving thoughts about *me*.

After looking at more artwork, Charli suddenly says, "I think you need a girl's night, Kate."

I turn towards her. "That would be great."

"Do you feel like watching a movie tonight at my house?" she asks casually. "We can eat chips and just veg out!"

My heart soars. I can hardly believe she has asked me this.

"Absolutely!" I say a bit too enthusiastically. "I mean, are you sure?"

She nods. "Trust me. I hate being alone in that house sometimes. It would be nice to have some company."

I am flattered that she even wants my company at all, and I suddenly find myself feeling shy again, like the first time I had seen her in thirteen years. What is going to come out of this night? Maybe Charli is just being nice, and maybe she's a little lonely, so of course she wants some company. That's probably why. However, deep within my chest, I am hoping there are other reasons she wants me to come to her house tonight.

Chapter 14

When I get out of my car and knock on her door, the cold air making me shiver, I see her dog in the window, barking at me. I'm not sure if it's the good "Yay, a human!" kind of bark or the "Get the hell away from my house" kind. Either way, I'm going inside.

Charli answers and I am taken aback. She has no makeup on her face and she changed into sweats, yet she still somehow manages to look gorgeous.

"Come in!" she says cheerfully, her eyes lighting up.

The dog has stopped barking and has come to sniff my ankles.

"That's Buster," Charli explains with a laugh. "Always interested in our guests."

I smile as she takes my coat. I look around at her house. It's modern, clean, and very tidy, which doesn't surprise me. What *does* surprise me, though, is the music blaring from the kitchen. As we walk closer towards it, I notice it is 80's pop music. I know the song, but I can't place what it is called or who sings it.

"I like 80s music," I say timidly.

"It was a good decade for music," she says with a sparkle in her eye. "Of course, I was very young in the 80's. Here, come sit!"

She walks me over to the living room area and, just like the rest of the house, it has a beachy sort of vibe and is very organized. In fact, everything is so clean it nearly sparkles.

I sit awkwardly on the couch, her coming to sit next to me but on the other side. I notice then the huge painting of the hummingbird on the wall, right where anyone can see it. She obviously put it up on her wall immediately, as I had not been far behind her when we were driving. Like the love I have for her, it shines in the most vibrant of ways.

"Oh, let me get the wine!" she says, standing up quickly and walking over to the kitchen.

I take another glance around. There are seashells on the windowsill and a beautiful blown-up picture of waves crashing on the shore behind me. The crown molding is white and the walls are a deep gray color, little glass figurines of sea animals gathered on a little table next to me. It really does feel like a beach house.

"Your home is lovely," I say in awe.

She comes back with two glasses of wine and hands me one.

"It's a lot cleaner now that my ex-husband is gone," she laughs, but she also has a subtle look of sadness on her face.

"Does it get better with time?" I ask. "The divorce?"

She sighs. "It does, Kate. It really does. I'm still in the grieving process a bit, but it gets easier every day. I know we made the right decision, even if it hurts."

I nod and sip the wine. Feeling shy, I tip the wine forward more and take a big gulp of it.

"So, Kate, what inspired you to write your beautiful story?" she asks, staring at me like she can see right through me.

I take a deep breath. "To be honest, nothing, really. I just had the idea come to me. That's how a lot of my stories are born. Something just pops into my head."

"Like electricity," she muses.

"Exactly," I say, surprised. "So, that happens to you, too?"

"Yes," she says. "Often."

"You have the biggest imagination," I say. "I'll never forget being a kid and reading your books. All those tales of goblins and witches and fairies. You got me soaked right up into that world you created.

I don't know how you do it."

She smiles. "Like you, sometimes things just pop into my head. I have to say, Kate, you write about romance so well. I never read anything like some of the love scenes you described."

I noticeably cringe this time. I don't even try to hide it.

"Why do you look so embarrassed?" she says, completely seriously.

I shake my head. "I'm- well, I know the sex in my book was a lot. I should probably cut most of it out."

"Why?" she asks. "Your book is for adults, and it's romance. If people can't handle it, they shouldn't be reading it!"

I try to smile but I frown. She notices and pours more wine into my now-empty glass. She really *can* read my mind.

"Charli," I say, afraid to ask but too curious not to, "what inspired you to write your book? I know you said that Melanie was a real person. I remember you saying she died from cancer when she was twenty-five. You don't have to tell me if you don't want to."

Charli sighs but nods. "I don't mind telling you, Kate. Yes, Sharon was a good friend of mine.

Everyone loved her. We all did. Just like in my book, Sharon was gorgeous, and caring, and sweet. She just lit everything up around her. I met her in college. She was my friend's roommate." There is a look that crosses her face of utter pain. It makes me want to reach out and touch her hand, but I resist. "I talked to her a few times and then we just started hanging out at all the parties. We became close very quickly. She was my best friend. When we were twenty-four, we decided to hang out on the beach and drink wine." Here, Charli pauses to sip her own glass of wine. "That part of the story when Violet and Melanie spend the night at the beach is true. That is what happened between Sharon and I. Just after that, when we started dating officially, she was diagnosed with cancer." I can tell that Charli is trying not to cry by the way her face is tense and she is biting her lip.

"You don't have to talk about it," I say softly, "if it's too hard."

"No, I want to," says Charli with determination. "I haven't talked about Sharon in so long. Probably because it really is so painful to think about. But I still want to keep her memory alive. She was so precious." Here, the tears start to come.

I can't help but scooch closer to her on the couch. Now, I lightly touch her arm.

"I'm sorry," she says, reaching for a tissue next to her. "It's been a long time since I've talked about Sharon. Thirty-two years since it all happened."

"Never apologize for that again," I say, placing my hand more firmly on her arm. "Never."

She looks at me gratefully. "Sharon's cancer progressed very fast. She was symptom-free for the longest time, and so once we found out she was sick, it was too late to save her." Charli took a deep breath. "She was diagnosed only days after that night on the beach. We were only together for seven months before she passed away. Like Melanie, Sharon also happened to die on her birthday. It was a very sad time for all of us."

I am shocked. For a second, I can't think of anything to say.

"She was a wonderful, special person," Charli continues. "When she passed, I put a hummingbird figurine inside the casket, since she loved them so much. My Sharon."

I am surprised when I find myself with tears rolling down my face. Charli notices and her eyes grow wide.

"Kate! I'm so sorry!"

"Don't apologize for your feelings," I tell her somewhat sternly. "Never. I'm glad you told me. Does it help to talk about her?"

She sniffles and nods. "It does. I feel very comfortable talking with you about it. Especially since you know a part of the story by reading my book."

"I'm happy you feel comfortable around me," I say, hoping that she never stops feeling comfortable with me. "I know Sharon is with you. I know she's proud of the book you wrote. Melanie is a beautiful character. You should be so proud of what you have written, Charli. So proud."

She looks over at me and smiles, showing her adorable dimples. This whole time, I have been trying not to stare at her. But now, it doesn't feel so strange to look into her eyes anymore. I think she is echoing this feeling, because she is staring into my eyes, too.

She suddenly reaches over the table, grabs the wine bottle, and pours herself another glass and tops mine off as well.

"Death is such a sad, scary thing," I say out loud. "Isn't it?"

Charli pauses to consider this statement. "Yes. But it is also a beautiful thing, too. Everyone must die, and the extinguishing of that life is very special. It's because time is so limited that it is so precious. That's why we shouldn't waste it. Not a second of it."

I look carefully into her eyes, trying to guess what she may be feeling. The wine has now made me feel a bit less inhibited and a lot more relaxed.

"Life is too short to waste it," I agree, putting my wine glass down on the table. "That's why I believe in telling people how I feel about them. That's why I'm so honest. I know it can come off unnerving, but it's just how I am. I'm sorry I creeped you out all those months ago- you know, when I told you I had feelings for you."

Charli looks at me and then frowns. "I'm not. I'm not sorry. I'm only sorry for how *I* reacted to it. I know I reacted poorly. I was hurt by you at the time, and my anger overcame me. I am sorry, Kate."

"If you are truly sorry," I say, "please don't apologize again. I hate to have hurt you. I can't even think about it without wanting to cry."

Suddenly, Charli looks over and gives me a curious look. "Kate. Why do you care about me so much?"

I shrug and say, "I can't explain it in words. I just do. I think I always have, but then I got to know you more through your story, and- well, I know you are not your story, but it's a piece of you, and I felt like I was reading your soul. I know that might not make sense."

Charli reaches out her hand and places it on mine. "It does make sense, Kate. It does."

"You have a beautiful soul," I can't help but add, watching her eyes begin to glow at me. I have never seen that look before, and I can feel goosebumps all over my body.

We stay silent for a moment, just staring at each other. It typically would be weird and awkward, but for some reason right now it isn't. In fact, I am feeling very chill. I gently pick up my wine glass, take a sip, and place it back down on the table.

"I suppose we should put on a movie," she says casually, picking up the remote. "Let's see what we have here!"

We both decide on a romcom, since it's a genre we both love, but I cannot pay attention to the movie. I am still sitting very close to Charli because I had not wanted to be rude by scooting back over to the other end of the couch. I thought that would make things more awkward than to just sit there.

I finish that next glass of wine, and don't ask when I pour another. Charli rejects a refill, and I realize that this has to be my last glass of wine; otherwise, I will begin to act stupid, and I cannot risk that around Charli. Charli has finally decided that I'm not actually crazy, and I can't ruin that again.

I am tipsy, though, which always makes me a lot more fearless and bolder. This time, I sneak glances over at Charli who, although so casually dressed and no makeup on her face, looks absolutely stunning, nevertheless. If anything, she's prettier without all the makeup. She just radiates natural beauty. It is hard not to look over at her, and I can't help it. She also looks a bit disinterested in the movie, too, and I can't help but wonder if she is feeling what I'm feeling.

Carefully, I move my body just an inch closer to hers so that she doesn't notice. Our arms touch slightly, and she doesn't pull away. I revel in the comfort of my long-sleeved shirt brushing up against her sweatshirt. Even just that touch is enough to make my head spin.

As the movie plays on, God knows what's happening, I make a bolder move by placing my hand next to me so that it is touching the side both of our thighs. I am very careful to do this slowly, mainly because I do not want to completely freak her out again.

I am in shock when she does the same. Now, our hands are lightly touching, our knuckles perfectly together. I reach my fingers out as if to stretch them and, by doing so, intertwine them with hers. I pull back innocently, but she suddenly weaves her fingers back through mine.

I inhale deeply. We are holding hands! I can hardly believe this is happening. I am hoping that my hand is not getting sweaty and clammy.

I suddenly have the guts to look over at her. When our eyes meet, she is staring right into my soul in that perplexing way of hers- that way that makes me feel like she's reading me. I can't look away. The wine has completely relaxed me now, but it isn't just that- Charli has a way about her that makes me feel so comfortable. Something about her feels like home.

I can feel myself tremble slightly. I don't know if I'm nervous or just in awe of what is happening.

Charli reaches over and picks up my hand with her other hand. I lean into her slowly, smelling her sweet-scented flowery perfume, and rest my head on her shoulder. She lightly rests our hands on her thigh and leans her head into mine. I lightly graze my thumb across her hand as she does the same to me. I can feel my blood pulsing in my body and the dizzy feeling coming into my head. We continue to "watch" the movie like that, but we are both wrapped up in each other's touch at that point.

The movie suddenly ends much too soon. I am so utterly disappointed. I don't want to lift my head from her shoulder, but I do. She seems reluctant as well and it takes her a moment to turn the TV off.

However, I don't move. Instead, I say, "I don't want to wear out my welcome, but- would you like to listen to music for a while? I mean, if you want to? I'm sorry, I just don't want to go home right now."

Her face glows and I am so relieved.

"Ok, but this time, *you* choose the song," she says, handing me her phone with her Spotify on which connects to a speaker in the kitchen. Then, she comes and sits down, right next to me, the way she was before.

I smile. I am so tempted to put on a song by Lana Del Rey, but I'm scared it will creep her out. Instead, I play "Pink" by *Leon*- beautiful, romantic, but not overdone. It is subtle, just like the way I am trying to be.

"That was a nice song," she says. "Ok, my turn."

She turns on another 80's song, and it is so romantic that I am blushing as I listen to it. My next song is "Five String Serenade" by *Mazzy Star*, which is heartfelt, enchanting, and painfully beautiful, just like the woman sitting beside me.

Charli is not hiding her feelings anymore. It is quite obvious now that she feels what I feel. Because I now know this, I bravely place my hand on hers. She doesn't flinch and looks over at me with that same admiring gaze. She moves a bit closer to me and we stare into each other's eyes. I am suddenly overwhelmed by the powerful love I have for her, and how much I desire her touch- and it's not just my body that wants it. It's also my soul.

I can feel my lips trembling and I can't look away. I don't know what to do now. I'm not really sure what she wants me to do. I don't want to be presumptuous, but I also don't want to miss out on an important opportunity.

Charli, however, decides for me. She lifts her hand and touches my face so lightly it feels like a feather running down my cheek. I momentarily close my eyes and breathe her in. I lean my face closer towards her and wrap my arm around her. In a moment, our noses are touching, and I can feel my hands shake. When I bring my lips towards her own, I reach for the back of her neck and lightly pull her towards me.

Kissing Charli is an experience I know I will never forget. It is unparallel to anything I have ever felt before. I drink her in, her gentle, soft lips covering mine, as she pulls me closer to her. We are now kissing more passionately than before, both of us throwing away any façade of polite shyness now.

"I thought I lost you forever," I whisper breathlessly.

"You'll never lose me again," she promises in that soothing voice.

I close my eyes and soak her in completely. My body feels almost numb now as I take her head in my hands and kiss her more aggressively this time.

She responds to my force with her own before suddenly standing up and taking my hand.

"Would you like to go upstairs?" she whispers in my ear when I am in front of her.

"Of course," I say, trying to catch my breath.

I walk behind her as she saunters carefully down the hall and to the stairs. When she gets there, she turns to me, grabs my head to kiss me, and then starts walking up. I can feel my whole-body quivering, both from nervousness and desire at once.

When we reach her bedroom, she takes my hand and leads me in so confidently that it catches me a bit off guard. I shyly look down at the ground, not sure what the hell I am expected to do next. Afterall, I have never been so close to a woman before in my entire life. I know what men want- they are so easy when it comes to their desires. But a woman? I have no idea what to do.

Sensing this, Charli takes me by my hand, starts kissing me softly again, and I don't protest when I reach towards the ceiling to let her take my shirt off. She kisses me more deeply than before and now my desire is overcoming any little timidness I have left.

Suddenly, the wine clouds my thought process, and I slightly push her against the wall. I then grab the back of her hair and kiss her aggressively as my hand grazes across her chest. I have imagined this moment so many times, yet actually having Charli's arms around me and her body pressed against mine is so much better than anything I could have conjured up in my imagination.

When she leads me towards the bed, I stand on my tip toes, sit, and then slowly pull her towards me. As I kiss her, I feel her warm body covering mine and her hand trailing slowly up my black stockings. I sigh with satisfaction when she begins kissing my neck and moving her hand up my thigh again. It is at this moment that everything around us goes dim and it is just Charli and me- two women who can finally be who they really are, two women who are now free to do as they please and show their love in any way they want. And, as our bodies form in complete alignment, I know I will never be able to turn back now.

Chapter 15

The next morning, I am expecting things to be pretty awkward. Instead, Charli wakes me up with a kiss on my forehead and a glass of orange juice. I sit up, a bit disoriented, and look over at her. She is very nonchalantly scrolling through her phone as if nothing happened between us. I momentarily am reminded of the way Melanie acted after she and Violet made love on the beach.

"Good morning!" she says suddenly, turning her head towards me with a big, lovely smile.

"Good morning," I say shyly, looking down at my hands.

As if she read my mind, she puts her hand to my face. "Did you want to talk about last night?"

I'm a bit flustered. I hadn't expected her to ask this. In fact, I expected her to freak out if anything and perhaps even regret the (incredible) night we spent together. Instead, it is as if she is completely comfortable around me.

I shake my head. "I don't think so. But-" I add, "it was nice. Last night. It was nice. Well, more than nice." I look at her and I just have to ask. "Was it nice for you, too?"

She answers me by cupping my chin in her hand and kissing me firmly on the lips.

"Better than nice," she states, so softly it's almost a whisper.

I sigh in relief. I sip the orange juice before quietly slipping my clothes back on, which is a bit awkward, but Charli is still looking into her phone intently.

"I should go," I say suddenly. "I have to get ready to see my friend."

In actuality, this isn't true, but I just strongly feel that I need to be alone right now to process what has happened between us. As much as I could spend the whole day with Charli, I know that I also need to ponder my next course of action and, honestly, take some deep breaths.

Charli looks concerned for a moment. "Are you ok, Kate? You can tell me honestly."

I lower my head, take her head in my hands, and kiss her. "I'm more than ok. I just have to see my friend. I'd rather stay here with you, though. Maybe, only if you want to, we can get together tomorrow? I mean, only if you want to."

Charli smiles her sweet smile again. "I more than want to," she says, "but tomorrow I'm attending a writer's conference up in Bergen County. What about Friday night? I know that's a long time away, but maybe we can go out to dinner or something, if you would like to."

I smile, probably looking more thrilled than I mean to.

"Of course," I answer.

"You're welcome here anytime, Kate," she says kindly. "Even on the weekdays. Just let me know you're coming, and I'll leave the door open for you!"

I am surprised at this offer. It is really very nice of her.

"You're always welcome at my house, too," I tell her. "My ex is going to stay with his friend in a couple days."

She says nothing but nods. Then, even surprising myself, I lean over and kiss her again. She's surprised too, as her eyes widen, but then she kisses me back more deeply and fully, pulling me right back down onto the bed.

"I can't even believe you were right this whole time," says Elena as we sip our coffee.

I gloat. "I told you we had a connection! I knew we did. I thought she might have feelings for me too, and I was right! I was right."

Elena raised her eyebrows. "So, are you guys, like official?"

As important as this was, I hadn't actually thought of that.

"Not really," I said. "At least I don't think so. Not yet, anyway."

"You better seal it," warned Elena. "Make sure she wants the same thing as you, otherwise someone is bound to get their heart broken. You do want an actual relationship with this woman, don't you?"

"Of course, I do," I answer, a bit snippier than I mean to. "I just hope that it's what she wants, too."

Elena raises her eyebrows. "How's lesbian sex?"

My mouth drops open, and my coffee almost flies out. "Elena!"

"Just wondering," she says with that usual sneaky look she has when she is being nosy about something.

I blush and put my coffee cup slightly in front of my face. "It's… well, it's definitely different."

"In a good way or a bad way?"

I know Elena can tell by my smile and the way I scrunch my face that it was definitely in a *good* way.

She starts to laugh and says, "Nice! I don't

know, Kate, but I'm starting to think you may have found the real thing. You know, the real deal. The *One*. I usually don't believe in that shit, but I'm getting strong soulmate vibes this time."

I can't help but gloat. I haven't been this happy in a very long time.

"You're right though," I say. "I need to ask her if she wants what I want. If she says no, well, it'll break my heart. I need to know sooner rather than later."

"I agree," says Elena, still looking at me in that sneaky way of hers.

"I just hope she wants what I want," I peep nervously.

My house feels a bit more cold and very empty now that Richie has moved out. Everything happened so fast, it's almost hard to believe.

At least I have Lila. She purrs sweetly in my lap as I scroll through TikTok. I am tempted to text Charli, but I am still so afraid I'll annoy her. I stop myself and sigh.

This has not been easy for me, and I do miss Richie, but I know that our separation was for the best. I cannot love him in the way he needs to be loved, and he cannot love me in the way I need to be loved, either. It was going to happen eventually-an inevitable pit we'd ultimately fall in. It just happened to occur sooner than I could have imagined.

I think of Charli, and I can't help but smile. I have truly won the prize of all prizes, the reward being her heart. If someone told me at eight-years-old that I would someday kiss my favorite author, I would not have believed it- for more than one reason.

Soon, my phone is buzzing. Crap. It's Charli and she's *calling* me.

I hesitate. I am so bad on the phone. I contemplate letting it go to voicemail, but my hand picks it up anyway.

"Hi Charli!" I say enthusiastically.

"Kate!" she says with equal gusto. "I know this is a bit out-of-the-blue, but I wanted to know if you would like to come with me to the hummingbird garden on Saturday."

My eyes grow wide. "You mean, there really is a hummingbird garden, just like in your story?"

"There is," she answers. "It's not well-known, and it's not super close, but there is one not too far from me. I was thinking it might be fun."

I jump up and down for a moment and I'm really glad Charli is not here to witness this burst of excitement.

"I'd love to," I say, trying to sound normal and not ecstatic. "What time?"

"Maybe we can meet at my house, and I'll drive!" she says cheerfully. "If you can get here at around noon, that might be a good time."

I am smiling so hard my cheeks hurt. "I'd love that."

"Great!" and that completes the conversation.

I lean down towards Lila and kiss the top of her head. She gives me a look as if to say, *what the hell is wrong with you*? And then I am already upstairs picking out the clothes I want to wear to the garden.

It is March now, and not quite as cold, but still cold enough that I don't want to wear a light dress. I eventually decide on a thicker red sweater dress and little black boots. I am tall enough as it is, so I wear my flat ones.

When Charli sees me, she puts her hands to her face. "You look beautiful!"

I feel electricity pulsing through my blood when she says that.

"You always look beautiful," I tell her.

Now that we have- well- *really* gotten to know each other, I no longer feel as awkward giving her compliments.

She surprises me when she leans over to kiss me before opening the car door for me.

"Let me see your Spotify," I say bravely as she hooks her phone up to her car.

She gives me a sly look but hands me her phone.

Her songs are definitely interesting with a lot of 80's and 90's hits. Then, as I continue to scroll, I see a whole bunch of Lana Del Rey songs. This time, I am not afraid to play one.

Young and Beautiful begins to play in the background and Charli starts singing the song. She is hardly singing though, and it is more like a hush whisper, yet it is so beautiful.

I look over at her in shock. I have never heard such a smooth, pure, and untainted voice before. She looks over at me and smiles.

"Is my singing annoying you?"

My eyes widen. "God no! Charli- I have never heard someone who can sing so well and whisper it at the same time."

She laughs and continues to watch the road.

"Please don't stop singing," I say. "You have the most beautiful voice I have ever heard."

She slightly blushes but begins singing again, sounding like a perfect angel. For a moment, I wonder in my head if that is, in fact, what she actually is- an angel in human form. An angel who has come to save me from my own self. An angel who has helped me to realize that I was living in pretend for so long, trying to be what society wanted me to be instead of who I really am. Charli, with all of her vivacity and flavor, has flown into my life at a time when I need her the most.

When we get to the hummingbird garden, I realize it is very much like the one she talks about in her book. It has a big hummingbird statue right on top of the wall when we go inside, just like in the story.

When we walk inside the greenhouse, I am blown-away. Hundreds of strikingly gorgeous hummingbirds fly throughout the leaves and the trees, some of them whipping by my head so fast that all I see is a blur of colors. Pinks, greens, purples, yellows, golds, even reds are zipping by all around me. One thing I did not expect were the little sounds echoing throughout the garden. Firm but gentle voices ring out like windchimes, and I am totally transfixed by their slightly high-pitched and cheerful music.

"The sounds they make are beautiful," I say

to Charli. However, Charli has walked away from me and is in another aisle, extending her arm out. I watch as a little hummingbird comes and lands right on top of her hand.

Charli's face lights up in excitement, those celestial-blue eyes of hers widening, and she looks over at me, her mouth open in surprise.

"That's amazing!" I cry as I slowly walk over towards her, careful not to disturb the bird.

The bird cocks their head to the side, looks over at me, and then spreads their wings, eventually meshing with the other birds so that we lose them in the crowd.

"This place is just…wow," is all I can think to say at that moment as brightly colored hummingbirds swirl around me, their graceful bodies hovering over the tall flowers, and their lovely voices ringing out such sweetness. It is a deeply sacred experience, and I find my eyes welling up with tears.

"Kate, are you ok?" Charli asks me with worry as she walks up beside me.

I wipe my one eye and nod. "I was just thinking of Violet and Melanie, and when Violet took Melanie to the hummingbird garden for her birthday. She didn't know that it would be the last day they would spend together."

Charli gives me a very sweet, sympathetic look and wraps her arm around me. The feeling of her anywhere near me is already enough to knock me off balance, but as I feel the warmth of her arm around my back, I get goosebumps all over my skin.

"I'm glad my story meant something to you," she says softly.

"It meant a lot more to me than I can describe in words," I tell her. "The way you write, with so much emotion, it's just- well, it's just magical, Charli. There's really no other word for it."

I turn around and take both of her hands in mine. We stare into each other's eyes, and I am suddenly unaware of anything else but the two of us, not even the hummingbirds. I am once again reminded that there is no one in the world like Charli Diaz, and I am lucky to spend even a mere moment in her presence.

Her gorgeous eyes light up even more, reminding me of an endless galaxy, as she squeezes my hands. "I'm happy you like it here. I really wanted you to see it. You would have loved Sharon, and she would have loved you, too. She would be happy to see that I took you here. She'd be happy for me that I found you."

I am honored that she has brought me to such a beloved place. We walk around a bit more, taking in the sweet-smelling nectar and the hummingbirds' lively songs. We are quiet for a while, just taking everything in, and when we turn to leave, one of the hummingbirds comes to land on my shoulder.

"Oh, Kate!" says Charli excitedly. "How amazing!

I giggle and try to keep still while Charli takes a picture. She is able to take it right before the elegant little bird lifts back off into the air again.

When we get into the car, she shows me the picture.

"Beautiful," she says with a sigh.

"I know, that hummingbird is gorgeous!"

"Yes, but that wasn't what I was referring to," she says, staring into my eyes. "I was talking about *you*."

I tap my foot on the ground, trying not to make it too obvious. Charli and I are sitting at her table, having dinner and drinking wine. She has cooked such an elegant meal of eggplant parmigiana and rotini and, as simple as it seems, it is delicious. I, however, can hardly eat. I need to know and I need to know now what is happening.

"You look like you want to say something," she says, narrowing her spectacular eyes at me.

"How did you know?" I ask her, honestly surprised as I thought my expression was totally neutral.

She chuckles. "I know you."

And, I realize that, despite not knowing me all that well, she really does *know* me. She *knows* my soul.

I sigh. I have already had a bit of wine in me so I am feeling brave.

"Charli," I say. "I want to know what I am to you. I mean, what we have. Like," I pause, trying to think of the right words. Instead, I suddenly blurt out, "I'm in love with you!" I actually hadn't expected to say that to her and my eyes grow wide with embarrassment. "I mean- I just-"

Charli reaches over to touch my hand. "Kate. I thought it was obvious. I'm in love with you, too!"

My mouth hangs open in what I imagine to be a very unrefined way.

"So, you want to be with me?" I ask her. "Together?"

Charli's eyes narrow as she casually sips her wine and smiles. "Yes, Kate. I do. I'm sorry, I thought it was obvious!"

"I overthink," I tell her. Suddenly, I realize I am gloating. "I'm happy to hear you say that. I'm happier than you can imagine."

We finish the rest of the dinner in silence. Usually, this would be awkward, but silence with Charli doesn't exactly feel quiet or tense. It feels normal, natural, and as if we are just soaking up each other's presence. Sometimes we steal glances at each other, and at one point I start to laugh.

"What's so funny?" she asks me gently.

The irony of the situation hits me again all at once. "We both trade books with each other, both about love and romance, and end up falling in love with each other! Isn't that a bit-"

"Serendipitous?" finishes Charli.

I nod and pat my mouth lightly with the napkin. We are about halfway through the meal, but I am full at this point. I also cannot think of eating, not now, not with everything we just confessed. Charli is staring at me with those eyes and I am totally transfixed. Her red lips look particularly tempting and her black nails begin to lightly tap the table as if she, too, is also impatient.

She keeps her gaze on me and I look away for a moment. When I look back, she is giving me the look she had given me right before we had gotten into bed that last time. I inhale quickly, feeling my heart start to beat frantically onto the wall of my chest. When she bites her bottom lip, I am completely in a trance.

I squirm in my seat like a child to try to distract myself, but Charli continues to keep her gaze on me. My hands begin to shake and I feel a heaviness- almost dizziness- in my head. I realize then that it is useless to try to refocus on something else.

"Are you finished eating?" she says in a completely calm and controlled voice.

"For now," I say with a nod.

She slowly stands up, saunters over to me, and reaches her hand out. I take it and stand, hoping she doesn't feel me trembling.

"Come," she whispers in my ear. This whisper only further stimulates me and I can do nothing but nod.

We slowly walk and she continues holding on to my hand as we go up the stairs. We just make it the landing when I grab her arm and pull her towards me. She pulls me in and kisses me back harder as I grab her face in my hands and brush her hair out of the way.

We cannot take our lips off of each other as we stumble into her bedroom. She kicks off her heels and I manage somehow to get my little boots off as she pushes me onto the bed. We are still fully clothed, and this only makes my desire build as she starts pulling my dress up past my thighs.

She leans over and kisses me, and we drink each other in for a while, our bodies pressed together. Everything around me goes dim and all I can concentrate on is the fire pulsing through my body and her hand squeezing mine. All of the sudden, I am in heaven. I am no longer on Earth anymore. I am one with the sky, the stars. Like a hummingbird, I am flying over myself and high above the clouds, soaring towards something unfamiliar but so natural for me. I begin making my own song as I cry out, bringing Charli towards me, the two of us tangled up in each other like the stems of two roses.

Lying there with Charli is something I could have only imagined in my wildest dreams. We stare into each other's eyes, not saying a single word yet saying everything on our hearts at the same time. My breathing is still a bit sharp, and my skin feels almost numb. The experience of making love to Charli is better than I could have ever imagined it being.

Instead of living in a cloud of façade, pretending to be what the world wants me to be, I am authentically myself. I no longer have to pretend to be straight. I can love and be loved in the way I have always meant to be. At the end of the day, it doesn't matter what other people say about us. Those strangers mean nothing to me. As long as Charli and I are together, that is all that really counts.

"I love you," I say to her, my voice hushed.

"I love you, too," she says as she snuggles closer to me.

With our arms wrapped around each other, we fall asleep like this, two hummingbirds who somehow found each other in this crazy, chaotic place called Earth.

Chapter 16

A month has gone by. An absolutely blissful month of just me and Charli together - going out to eat, sleeping in, watching movies, visiting shops, and spending as much time as possible with each other. I relish every moment we get to spend together, and I hate those times when we both have to part, like when I go off to work or she goes to a writer's conference. We know these are necessary life occurrences, but they suck nevertheless.

"Let's go to the beach today," she says on a Saturday morning as we wake up from the sun beating down on us through the window. "It's supposed to be perfect."

"Won't it be a bit cold?" I ask, for it is only April.

"It's supposed to get sunnier," she answers. "Let's bring sweaters and wine. Although, I must say, we drink far too much wine!"

I roll over and cup her chin in my hand. "Maybe we can do what Violet and Melanie did when they went to the beach."

"Not in broad daylight," she laughs, giving me a kiss and standing up.

The air feels light and there is a colder breeze, but Charli is right. It gets much sunnier as soon as we are on the sand. This time, Charli chooses a little beach about twenty minutes away since there are less people, and it is more peaceful.

Charli spreads a blanket out while I grab the wine from my knapsack. We pour it into little wine glasses and cheer to the day.

"I'm so happy the weather is getting warmer," I say cheerfully. "Aren't you?"

"Oh, definitely," she answers, smiling as she looks up into the sky.

Everything she does mesmerizes me and I continue to stare at her. She notices and wraps her arm around me.

"My Kate," she says cheerfully. I smile. I'm *her* Kate now.

"All I've ever wanted is you," I tell her as I lean my head on her shoulder and touch her arm.

She kisses my forehead and holds me closer. Suddenly, she slides over and I notice the stunned expression on her face.

"What?" I ask, looking around. "Is there a ghost I should be aware of?"

"Look," she says, her voice soft.

I look over in her direction and there, in all of

their colorful glory, is a hummingbird, green and blue. They fly a bit closer and hover around our blanket, dipping forward and back in that way hummingbirds often do, their body vibrating, and their long beak stretched out towards us.

"Wow," I say in awe. "How beautiful."

We watch them fly around us for a moment, admiring their flamboyant plumage, before they take off.

"This is what Violet saw when she thought of Melanie!" I cry, touching Charli's hand excitedly. "What do you think this means for us?"

Charli smiled. "I like to think it means that Sharon is giving us her stamp of approval. She would have just loved you. I wish the two of you could have met. She would be very happy for me that I found you, she really would. I also think it means that you and I have something really special."

I sigh. "I really like that interpretation." We continue to sit for a while until I say mysteriously. "Let's do what they did."

"What do you mean?" she asks me.

"Let's grab some dinner and then come back here," I say. "Then we can sip some more wine and sleep on the sand. Come on. Why not?"

Charli gives me a sly half-smile and I know that the answer is a yes. This is one of the things I love about her. She is adventurous- even more so than I am- and is always ready to do something completely absurd.

After dinner, we return to the beach. Now, there are no people, and the blue sky is swirling with orange and pink clouds. The breeze has picked up a bit, but we are in longer sweatshirts now and so we don't feel the cold.

"There's nothing like the sea!" she exclaims in such a vivacious voice that you might have thought she was a kid again.

She extends her arms towards the sky and spins around, much like I had pictured Melanie doing in the story. Her feet splash in the water and her golden hair shines in the sleepy sun. The bottom of her pastel-blue dress rises around her legs as she continues to spin around, so much so that she nearly makes me dizzy, although it does not seem to bother Charli a bit. She is a perfectly radiant sight, and I completely forget that the woman is pushing sixty.

When she comes back to sit next to me, her whole face is glowing with joy.

"There's nothing like the beach to inspire me," she says happily. "Why don't you join me?"

I give her a look. "I don't think so."

"Don't be a loser!" she teases, lifting me up off the ground.

And then she proceeds to drag me into the ocean, my ankles practically getting frost bit from the cold water, as she spins me around. In a moment, we are laughing, and I am awkwardly trying to dance with her. The woman can actually dance- I mean *really* dance, and I struggle to even move my feet. Charli beams like a ray of sunshine and I am captivated by her once more. She is just so simply *herself*, all the time, in every way. It's admirable that someone can just be themselves without worrying about what anyone thinks. This is one of the things I like most about Charli.

"I'm not the best dancer," I say as I laugh into her arms.

She laughs with me and grabs onto my waist as waves crash beside us, knocking us over so that we're flailing around in the water.

Still cracking up, we head back up to the blanket and pick at our cupcakes, watching as the sun fades away in the distance and the stars peek out from behind the sky.

I am suddenly painfully reminded of those bad times months ago when Charli and I were fighting.

"Charli?"

"Yes?"

"Do you ever think about...you know, back when we were angry with each other?" I ask with trepidation. "Do you ever think about it and still feel angry?"

Charli gives me a sincere look. "Kate. What happened was really bad. It was emotional for me. But we've put that in the past. I know that your insults were not really directed to me, but more directed to the pain you went through, and vise versa. Yes, sometimes very rarely it pops up in my head, but no, Kate, I never feel angry with you."

I sigh in relief. "I feel the same way."

She leans her head on my shoulder, and I lean mine on top of her head. We stare out into the ocean, watching as the little mountains of water rise and foam over, the sky now beginning to darken.

"The ocean makes me sad," I say. "Not in a bad way, though. It just reminds me of how nothing really lasts. Do you ever feel that way when you sit by the ocean?"

Charli pauses to contemplate this. "I have before, definitely. But as you get older, you're also reminded of how delicate and fragile life is. Yes, it doesn't last forever, but when I see the ocean, I am reminded of how some things *do* last."

"Like love?"

"Like love," she agrees, lifting her head and staring into my soul.

"Your eyes have some kind of power over me," I admit with a little laugh.

"What kind of power?" she asks. "I hope it's a good one!"

Instead of answering, I lean over to kiss her. I drink her in, feeling the electricity run through my body as she pulls me closer. Ignoring the sound of hungry seagulls, we continue to kiss, now falling back onto the blanket.

"I never thought I'd meet anyone like you, Kate," she says to me when we part lips.

I place my hand on hers. "I feel that way about you. I can't imagine how I've lived my whole entire life without you. It kills me to even think about it. Imagine if we didn't forgive each other. Imagine how lonely we'd both be."

"Yes, but we *did* forgive each other," she says softly. "That's what's important."

Suddenly, without warning, I start to cry. Charli sits up quickly in an effort to comfort me.

"I begged the Universe to bring you back to me," I sob. "I tried a hundred ways to manifest you, Charli. I didn't give up hope that you would return to me someday."

The look on Charli's face then is so sincere that I just want to take a picture of her so that I can keep it forever.

"I did, too," she says, her own eyes beginning to water. "I asked the Universe for you to come back to me, too. I promised I would never take you for granted again. Not ever."

We kiss again, and this time we don't stop for a long time. When we finally do look up, the sky is even darker than it was before.

"Let's sip some more wine and tell secrets," I say in a casually sneaky voice.

"Secrets?" she laughs. "I've got one for you—there is sand all over my ass!"

We both laugh and I playfully hit her arm.

"I'm serious," I say. "I want to know everything about you, Charli. Tell me anything and everything!"

Pouring more wine into our little glasses, Charli sighs. "What do you want to know?"

"Like I said, everything. Let's start with how you grew up."

Charli details her life and growing up, as I listen and try to picture Charli as a little kid. It isn't too hard to do since she is already filled with such youthfulness. The way she talks is so full of life and her eyes seem to grow deeper and brighter as she goes on. She talks about high school, college, and more about her former girlfriend, Sharon.

"She meant the world to me," Charli says. "I couldn't stop crying when she was diagnosed with cancer. It was the worst news I have ever heard in my entire life. You would have loved her, Kate. She was so energetic and *so* funny! Everyone loved my Sharon. But I loved her the most."

I bite my lip to keep the tears at bay. "I'm so sorry you lost her."

Charli gives me a sad look and then says, "Which loss has been the hardest for you?"

I suddenly feel sick. My hand clutches the blanket and I look out onto the horizon, which is growing darker and darker.

"My brother, Ted, died when he was twenty," I say quietly. "I was thirteen."

Charli reaches out and touches my hand. "I am so sorry. Were you two close? You must have been."

I sigh and look away. I absolutely hate discussing this topic, but I have made Charli tell me all of her most treasured secrets, so I feel I owe her this.

"No," I answer flatly. "We weren't close at all."

I know this is a surprise. I glance over at her, and she is giving me a look as if to say, *Ok? Keep going.*

"When I was eleven and my brother was eighteen, he sexually assaulted me." I watch Charli's face turn from curious to horrified. "It was bad at the time, and my parents even pushed me into therapy. Therapy helped a lot. My therapist was awesome. But the event still took a toll on me. I was so young, and I felt so hopeless and scared. I stopped talking in school for the rest of that year. I was in fifth grade. My brother ended up going to jail for a while. He apologized to me a year later, but I didn't forgive him. I'm not sure I forgave him even when he died. I'm not sure I ever will."

Charli holds me close to her. She doesn't say anything for a moment. Then, she looks at me and says, "I'm a writer, Kate, but I am at a loss for words. I can tell you that what happened to you is terrible, but you already know that. I am beyond sorry, Kate. If there is something further than sorry, that is what I am feeling. I would take it all away for you, if I could."

I place my hand on Charli's. "It helps just to talk about it. Besides my best friend, Elena, I've never told anyone outside of my family except my therapists. I'm surprised, but it actually really did help to talk to you about it."

I notice tears in the corner of Charli's eyes as her lips begin to tremble.

"Kate," she says as she starts to cry.

I pull her close towards me and kiss the top of her head. We watch the waves get darker as we hold each other, silently taking in the night, saying things with our mind that we don't have to say out loud. This is because we inexplicably know each other without having to say a word. I can feel her thoughts through her skin, sense her feelings through her eyes, and know her soul by her mere aura.

"I would like to go back to the hummingbird garden," I say, digging my toes into the sand.

"We will," she says softly. "We can go anywhere we want."

Anywhere we want.

"I've never loved someone so much as I love you," I say suddenly, even surprising myself.

Charli leans more into me and whispers, "Kate, you will always be my greatest love."

"You don't have to say that," I say quickly, remembering her Sharon. "Please don't."

But Charli is calm when she replies. "I love Sharon and I always will. But I didn't expect you to come crashing into my world like this. You have brought life and trust into my life. There is no one like you in this world. I'm so happy to be with you. Happy isn't even the word. I'm a writer, and I still cannot describe in words how much I love you.

"I want to be with you forever," I say, my breath hushed in the wind. "Do you want the same? I need to know."

Charli looks at me with a visage of pure devotion. "I do. I do want the same."

I respond by kissing her again.

"Maybe we can get married in the hummingbird garden," I muse. "That would be so beautiful, wouldn't it? Imagine all of the colorful birds flying around us."

"It may not be so romantic when they poop on our heads." Charli has a point and we both begin to laugh.

"Charli?" I ask. "Can you sing for me again?"

Charli gives me a doubtful look but then relents when I pout my lips. She begins singing such a sweet song that it nearly makes me tear up. It is a song I've never heard before and I am in a complete trance from the majestic sound of her voice. I have never heard anything so beautiful before.

As she sings, I am reminded of the hummingbirds and their striking beauty. And, just like them, Charli sings to me, her voice echoing through my mind like a prayer. It is the perfect lullaby- the one that I have been waiting my whole life to hear.

After she sings, we spend the rest of the night under the blanket, enjoying each other's love, finding comfort and solace in our embrace. And, like two hummingbirds, we fly away from the outside world and become wrapped up in our own colors, making up our own special song, forgetting about all other worries and cares. Afterall, we have each other now. And that is the greatest lullaby of all.

Chapter 17

I have never, in my entire life, been happier. Work, which still is a drudge, is a bit more bearable now that I can talk to Manny and Rian about my girlfriend. Home, which is sometimes still eerily quiet, doesn't bother me so much since either Charli is there or I am at Charli's. I have even begun taking Lila with me over to her house, and she and the dog have formed quite an interesting bond where they lay together and take turns licking each other. I have never seen a cat and dog behave like that together before. It is almost as if they are soulmates, too.

Going to work from Charli's is not so bad, although it is a bit of a drive, and I ignore Charli's insistence that she stay over my place more. This is because, although I love it when she comes over, I would rather be in her house- where her positive energy glows everywhere, through the walls and into the air, where I can feel her everywhere, where all of her things and pictures and memories are. I relish at being at Charli's house and have practically a whole new set of toiletries and clothes just for her place.

It is now the middle of the summer and I have decided to have a party at my house. Well, more of a gathering, since it will literally be just me, Charli, Rian, Manny, and Elena. However, it is the closest thing I have had to an actual party since Richie used to bring all of his friends over, and I am so excited for Charli to meet everyone, and for them to meet Charli.

I am anxious as I put on my airy pink dress made of chiffon over my head and fasten it with its matching lacy belt. Charli likes this dress on me because she says it makes me look like a fairy. Even though I don't love this light pink color with my red hair, I wear it because Charli is obsessed with this look.

I highlight my eyelids with green eyeshadow to match my eyes and be sure to put my thin gold bracelet around my wrist along with my dangling gold earrings. I smooth my lips over with light pink gloss and throw on my little pink flats. I am so excited for everyone to meet each other.

Elena arrives first in her very boho sundress.

"Where's your guest of honor?" she asks me with her sneaky smile.

"Charli's on her way," I say, taking out my phone and snapping a quick selfie of us. "She had a writer's group meeting earlier today."

Elena took out her phone to snap another selfie. It is at this moment that Manny and Rian walk in.

Rian is looking perfect, as usual, and wearing a white crop top with little yellow booty shorts. Rian is much younger than the rest of us thirtysomethings, and at only twenty-seven, she can rock a lot more outfits than I can.

"Hey babe!" she says, rushing over and embracing me. "Where can I put this?"

She holds a platter of chocolate-covered pretzels in her one hand, and I take it from her, placing it onto the kitchen table behind me.

"I cannot wait to meet your lady," says Manny enthusiastically, giving me a hug and nearly knocking me over.

As usual, Manny is dressed head to toe in black, as is his typical style in general. He always says that he looks "bomb in black" and takes this very seriously.

"I hope you guys like her," I say nervously.

"I'm sure we will," says Rian, always so sweet, her bright blonde hair framing her round face perfectly and her perky boobs popping out of the crop top.

"Who wants wine?" I ask cheerfully, grabbing some pinot grigio from the counter. I struggle to open it and everyone laughs at me.

"Let me, girl," says Manny, coming over and dramatically popping the lid off.

It's at this moment when I hear the door open and close. Charli is here.

When she enters the kitchen, everyone awkwardly waves and says hi. Instead of being awkward back, Charli's eyes widen brightly, and she smiles warmly, bringing a ray of sunshine into the kitchen. She is wearing a floral shirt with tight white shorts and red heels. She looks like summer itself.

"Wow!" she says enthusiastically. "It's so great to finally meet all of you!"

She hangs her purse up on the chair and my other friends all stare at her.

"When you said she was fifty-eight, this isn't what I expected," Elena says to me in a normal voice. Typical Elena. Just saying anything that pops into her damn head.

Obviously, everyone has heard her including Charli. It only makes Charli laugh.

"I hope it's a compliment!"

Elena breaks out into a smile. "You're really hot, actually!"

"Girl, you are *super* hot," adds Manny, coming over and giving her a once-over. "*Damn*, Kate! If I was straight... well, you'd have some competition."

I can't even believe this is the introduction Charli is getting from my friends. How embarrassing.

However, Charli is totally unfazed. She blushes and laughs, her eyes lighting up. I wonder if there has ever been one single awkward bone in her body, because all I have seen of her so far is her exuding confidence.

"You didn't tell me your friends were all so beautiful," Charli says, giving everyone another smile.

"I like her already!" says Manny as he pours her some wine. "Have some of this, honey."

Charli takes the glass and then we all pour the wine into our glasses, holding it up and cheering.

"To new friends!" cries Elena.

"To new friends!" the rest of us say, all of us taking a big sip.

We then sit down at the little table and start eating cheese and crackers, potato chips, and chocolate-covered pretzels while my friends quiz Charli on nearly everything. Charli answers everyone's questions with a level of calmness and grace that is admirable. Now and then, we meet each other's gaze and neither of us can help but grin. Her smile is so contagious and no matter how many times I see it, it still sweeps me off my feet.

"Our girl has good taste," says Manny. "Well, besides Richie."

"Stop, Manny!" I chide. "Richie's still a friend!"

"Sorry," he mumbles, but gives Charli a look as if to say, *no way*.

"We love her. Kate is such an awesome girl!" says Rian with excitement. She is, by far, the sweetest person I know, because "awesome," isn't exactly a word I would describe myself as.

"You were married before, right?" Elena asks Charli casually, sipping her wine.

Charli nods. "I married a man and spent most of my life with him, but it just didn't work out. We still love each other and we're still friends, but it was better that we separated."

Elena nodded in understanding. "Me and my ex are like that."

"What about all of you?" asks Charli. "I'd love to hear more about each of you!"

And then it is a contest to see which friend will beat each other to it first. Manny wins, of course, and starts gabbing on and on about his many exes and how each of them had betrayed him in some way or another. Then it is Elena's turn to go on and on about her own ex and how the sex was great, but they were both emotionally unavailable.

Rian finally gets a chance to get a word in edgewise and talks sweetly about the job at the bank, how close she is with her dad, and then her fiancé Ryan, and how funny it is that they have the same name but two different spellings. Charli does a great job listening and answering questions. I think in my head that she could be a therapist by just how well she is able to capture what everyone is saying and respond in an empathic manner.

My friends clearly love her, and when we start playing "Cards Against Humanities," they find Charli's cards absolutely hilarious. In fact, they all seem to have completely forgotten about me as they swoon over Charli and crack up at her jokes. Charli really does have a way of hypnotizing everyone.

By the time the bottle is empty, and the cards are splayed out on the table, everyone is hanging on to Charli's words like glue. It is clear that we can sit here all night, but it's been hours and it's getting late. Also, I am very much desiring to get Charli alone so that I can have her all to myself.

"Alright," I say, standing up. "I'm getting so tired, guys. I'm sorry."

"I should get going anyway," says Rian. "Ryan and I are supposed to watch a movie."

"Ugh, I guess I need to take the hint and go," says Elena with a sigh. "We'll leave you two to…"

"Don't, Elena," I warn her, giving her one of my classic looks.

"What? I was going to say that we'll leave you two to clean up the kitchen and get some rest!"

"Sure," I laugh, shaking my head.

"Girl, we have got to get together another time!" exclaims Manny, taking Charli's hands and kissing each one of them. "Babe," he says to me, "you chose a good one."

I'm glowing. They all like each other! And Charli did such a good job making them feel comfortable.

We say our goodbyes and then it is just Charli and me.

"What did you think?" I ask, nervous for what she may say. "I know they're a little crazy."

Charli smiles. "They're adorable! I love them."

"They seem to love you, too," I say. "But I'm happy they're gone. Let's watch something together. I've been wanting you all to myself all night now."

Charli gives me a mischievous look, as if she has something else under her sleeve, and she, out of nowhere, pulls me close to her and plants a kiss on my mouth. I kiss her back and we continue to do this until we are somehow able to make it to the couch. Once again, I am reminded of how lucky I am to have Charli in my life, especially now.

Chapter 18

"I can't believe it," Charli says excitedly, staring at the letter in her hand.

It is another summer day, and Charli and I are about to go to an outdoor Tiki bar when Charli notices the big envelope hanging out of the mailbox.

"What is it?" I ask, coming around to look.

The letter reads:

"Dear Charli Diaz,

You are cordially invited to the Best Authors of the Jersey Shore banquet on August 7th, beginning at 7pm, at Gibson Hall on Route 9. Your latest novel, Shipwreck, *has been selected as a nominee in this competition. It is encouraged that you wear your best attire, as the winner will make a speech in front of the audience. Please have a speech prepared in case you win. Through this award, money will go to your charity of choice. It is encouraged that you consider which charity you would like the donations to go to and respond to the link at the bottom of this letter. This is a crucial step, as we need to know where to send the prize money to. The prize money consists of $20,000, so choose wisely.*

You are permitted to bring one guest. Please respond to the link with the name of the person you are bringing to this event. Dinner and dessert will be included, and please respond to the link with the meal you would like, as there is more than one option.

We look forward to seeing you. Please remember to RSVP as soon as possible.

- Jersey Shore Authors Society"

"I have always wanted to do this, Kate," Charli gushes, her whole face lit up like a candle. "The Jersey Shore Authors Society is a big deal. They promote a lot of books. I submitted mine just for fun. I can't believe I got chosen to be one of the contenders. I won't win, of course, but just being there will be such an honor."

"Charli," I begin, "I am so happy for you! Words can't even express it. You deserve this. You've worked so hard. You've earned it. And don't say that you're not going to win- you don't know that for sure! Oh, this is so exciting, let's go dress shopping! Wait- are you going to bring me?"

Charli purses her lips. "I was thinking of inviting someone else. Yes, Kate, of course I'm bringing you, who else do you think I'd bring?"

I brighten. "After the Tiki bar, we are going to the outlets. We are going to buy you the most gorgeous dress there is!"

The joy on Charli's face is so contagious. I can't help but smile. I am so proud of her.

The next week seems to fly by. When it is time for the special banquet, I feel like I just blinked, and it is here already.

Charli and I get dressed up to the nines. Charli is always beautiful, but she looks particularly stunning tonight. It isn't just her hair which is curled at the top of her head, or her mascara-dripped eyelashes, or her wine-red lips that do it, but it is also her happiness that seems to glow up everything around her.

She decided to buy a gorgeous royal-blue silk dress with matching heels and accented silver jewelry, while I picked a long, purple dress with a gold belt and gold flats. I would never wear heels to such an event, as I would just simply tower over Charli, and I'm tall enough as it is.

"Are you nervous?" I ask her, for I myself am feeling jittery.

She nods. "Terrified."

"Well, don't be," I say. "You look beautiful, you have a speech prepared if you win, and we're about to get free tiramisu. What can be better than that?"

She smiles as we jump into my car.

I can tell that she's nervous because she doesn't say anything the entire way there except to point out directions. When we get there and have the car parked, there is a huge crowd of people standing in the front, all wearing their best clothes.

"Do you know any of these people?" I ask Charli.

"No," she says. "Not a single one of them."

When we walk into the hall, I am immediately blown away by the marble-floored foyer and the humungous chandelier on the ceiling. Everyone looks happy and are talking excitedly amongst each other. Some of them appear to know each other very well, and I feel a bit out of place. Many stare at us as we walk forward. We are holding hands, so I'm not surprised we are being stared at, but I am a bit uncomfortable with some of the unapproving looks a few of the people give us.

One of them includes an older lady- maybe in her seventies- with gray hair in a tight bun. She looks at our faces, down at our hands, and purses her lips, giving us a very disapproving scowl.

Since "coming out," I have felt totally comfortable with being myself. However, it is moments like these that remind me how much my life has changed. What people who are not in the LGBTQ+ community do not understand is that "coming out" isn't just a one-time thing for us. We have to do it over and over and over again. To our families, to our friends, to strangers we meet, and to the public nearly every day.

People in straight relationships do not understand how much same-sex or multi-sex couples have to be careful. When I was with Richie, it was easy. We wanted to go on a trip? Cool. We'd book a room with one queen-sized bed without being questioned. We wanted to kiss in the park under the snowy trees? Easy. We just leaned forward and did it. We wanted to hold hands at the movies? Ok!

Now, although Charli and I certainly have these options, we have to be more careful about the places we visit, who we confide in, and where we express our love publicly. We can't be so thoughtless. Even today, people are judgmental and ignorant, and we have to remember that. I never realized just how difficult this would be. It is all worth it a million times though, as anything is worth going through for Charli.

Now, a couple of men in red ties graciously lead us to our table in the enormous banquet room, and then we sit. At the table with us is about five other people who look almost as uncomfortable as we do.

"At least we're not the only ones who don't know anyone here," I whisper to Charli.

I look around at all of the tables. There are so many people here that it is daunting. Many of them are much older than me, and look around Charli's age. However, some of them look as young as teenagers. This makes me a bit jealous, as I'm now thirty-three and have never been selected to possibly win such a grand award. Yet, a seventeen-year-old is in the running. I try to be happy for the kid, but I can't help but feel a little green.

It is very noisy; so noisy, in fact, that I barely hear the man come up on stage and introduce himself. Once he does that, though, everything falls eerily quiet, as if we were listening to a funeral procession.

"I thank you all for attending this banquet tonight," the man says with a big smile. "So many people here, of all different ages and backgrounds. That's the great thing about writing, isn't it? It brings so many different people together."

At that, Charli reaches over and holds my hand. I am expecting her to squeeze it and let it go, but she does not. Instead, she holds it steadily. Then, she whispers in my ear, "Are you ok that I'm holding your hand in here?"

Ok? Was she serious? I was more than ok- in fact, I was actually hoping people would notice.

I answer by holding her hand more tightly as the man on the stage continues to discuss the society, why the society began, and all of the successful banquets before it. Eventually, we break our grip when the waitress comes and brings us water and bread.

"Now, we are going to announce the winners of the Best Authors of the Jersey Shore," the man goes on, still smiling like he is in a dental commercial, his teeth so white that my eyes hurt from all the way across the room. "After we have done that, we will continue with the main course before dessert. Before we get started, I must announce that every single one of the authors in this room should be proud of themselves. All of you are here for a reason. You wrote something so great that you have enhanced the lives of others, as well as the Jersey Shore Authors Society. All of you deserve to be here. For those that do not win awards, just know that you are incredible and deserve success. With that, let's get started."

I look over at Charli and smile, clapping with the rest of the people. It is obvious how nervous she is, as she is biting her lower lip, which she usually only does when feeling vulnerable.

"Will you still love me if I don't get nominated?" she asks me.

"I will love you even if you win the award for the worst writer in the world," I laugh, "which would never happen."

This makes Charli smile and I can tell she feels more at ease.

"I know I'm not going to win," she whispers, "but for some reason, I'm nervous. I have no idea why."

I squeeze her hand as the announcer begins announcing.

He goes through three honorary mentions, giving each of them a big check for their charity and a big award in the shape of a golden pen, and then the big numbers begin.

When he announces third place, and it isn't Charli, she visibly relaxes.

"Thank God," she says, taking a sip of the water. "As disappointing as it is, I'm ok with this. I really didn't want to go on stage anyway."

I don't pay her any mind because there are still two places left.

By the time he calls the second-place winner, Charli is already on her phone. I can tell that she has completely and totally given up on winning this thing. But I haven't. Although Charli is so hard on herself, I know just how much of a special person she is, and just how good her writing is.

"Now, for the moment we've all been waiting for," continues the announcer. "The winner of the Best Authors of the Jersey Shore competition! After writing a beautiful book that has touched many lives, the voting has come in, and it is my humble honor to announce that the winner of this prestigious competition, and of the prize- which consists of a whopping $20,000 to be donated to a charity of choice- is..."

I can't help but roll my eyes. This guy is a little bit overdone.

"... Ms. Charli Diaz. Come on up, Ms. Diaz!"

I turn towards her and begin clapping wildly. I place my hands on hers and squeal in excitement.

"Oh my God, Charli!" I cry. "You did it! You won! You won first place!"

The look on Charli's face is priceless. Her mouth is hung open and her eyes are wide. She looks at me and whispers, "I didn't think I'd win. I don't have my speech."

"Where the fuck is it?"

"In the car," she says.

Then, knowing she has to do something as all eyes are on her now, she slowly stands up and gives the audience a big smile.

There she is. There's Charli- nervous and uneasy on the inside, but so confident and full of ease on the outside.

I shout out like I'm at a rock concert. I am so unbelievably happy for her.

Charli, in her usual composed manner, walks up the stage, her back straight as an arrow. She smiles, once again lighting up the entire banquet hall, and I am mesmerized by her. She looks so beautiful, and I think to myself how much I don't deserve a woman like that.

"I am honored," she says as she takes the mic. "Wow. I'll be honest, I did not think I was going to win tonight. I did write a speech, but I left it in the car." At this, she laughs as does the rest of the hall. She can charm anyone. "So now, I'm forced to make a speech that comes directly from my heart."

She looks over at our table and gives me a smile. "The purpose for writing *Shipwreck* was to explore the ways people can get stuck when they love someone. Sometimes, when we are in love, we can get ourselves into quite a bit of trouble." Here she pauses to smile, and the audience chuckles. "I think we can all relate to that on some level.

"When I first started writing the book, I was pretty skeptical," she continues. "I was just getting a divorce and I felt like I really was on a ship that had ruined its sail. I felt alone and lost, and had nowhere to go. That is why the book is a bit grim. As much as I think the message of being lost in love is powerful, and how it can cause extreme suffering, I have changed my mind about the ending of the book a bit.

"If I were to write it now, I would add a little something at the end." Here, she looks at me. "Love is scary and messy and even sometimes broken. However, where would any of us be without it? My heart had become cold and bitter. I swore off love for a while. But then I got to know this woman. She was brave and courageous enough to tell me how she felt about me. She opened my eyes and made me see that it was possible to love again. Not only love but love someone I would have never expected to in the first place." Here, she looks as if she is about to cry, and it takes everything in me not to stand up and run to her. "If I were to write the book again, instead of the character being lost alone on the island forever, I would bring another ship in to save their life. I would have the sailor find the character and make it all worth it, even the struggles. And that is what my love has done for me. I will always be thankful for Kate McMullin, who showed me what it's like to not be shipwrecked alone."

With that, most of the audience stands up and claps, some people looking in my direction. There are some faces in the audience that look a bit uncomfortable, as if they have never heard of two women loving each other before, but, for the most part, her speech is well-received.

I am the proudest person in the whole room. I stand up and continue to shout and clap like a madwoman as Charli holds the huge check in front of her and takes pictures for the camera. She has decided to donate her money to a local LGBTQ+ organization geared towards education and understanding of the community. She will be in newspapers and magazines throughout the country. I am not surprised that she won, but I am surprised at how gracefully she has accepted this award. It is admirable.

She eventually comes down to sit next to me, all eyes on us now. And when she does, she whispers, "Is it ok to kiss you here?"

I answer by putting my hand on her face and planting a kiss on her lips.

Dinner is nice, nothing too special, but the tiramisu is excellent, and I eat far too much of it. Charli and I, despite others being at our table, are in our own little world. I cannot stop smiling and she laughs at me, telling me I'm being ridiculous and there is nothing to be proud of. I tell her to mind her business and that she is the most fascinating person I have ever met.

When we finally get up to leave, and we are walking towards the parking lot, a few men in suits come up to us. They look to be in their late-forties-fifties, and by the looks on their faces, I can tell that they are not coming up to congratulate Charli.

"Hey, sexy," says one of the men, putting his hand around Charli's waist.

She looks shocked, and I immediately turn around and hold her hand so that the guy gets the picture. She is *my* love.

"This one's not too bad either," says another man, coming up to me and putting his hand on my ass. "Actually, you're way too hot to be a lesbian."

I am shocked. Charli looks just as mortified as I do. I pull her hand and we continue walking to the car, this time at a much faster pace. However, the four men continue to follow us.

Of course, we had to park all the way in the back, as we had gotten there late, and now we have so much walking to do.

"Where you ladies going?" asks another one with a scar across his eyebrow. "It's not so late. Maybe we can all do something."

"We're tired," I reply icily, gripping Charli's hand more tightly.

The men begin to laugh, and the fourth one puts his arm around my waist as another one does the same to Charli. I hastily look around me to see if I can call for help, but there is no one. Just the dark parking lot and the moon above our heads- and these creepy guys.

"Please don't touch me," Charli says as she wiggles out of the man's grip.

"Oh, don't we have a bold one here," he says, sneering at her. I want to punch him in the face. "Come on, girls. Let's go out. You can tell us all about your book. I'd love to read it."

I purse my lips and free myself from one of the man's arms. "Leave us alone. Now."

"Spicy," says one of them. "I like them spicy."

"Spicier the better," agrees another.

Charli and I look at each other and the fear on her face is so evident. It makes me want to vomit all over these men, the way they're making her feel.

We are now walking so fast we're practically in a jog. The men continue to follow us as we pick up our speed. It is hard for Charli to walk in her heels, and at one point she trips, falling into the arms of one of the creeps.

"If you wanted me, baby, all you had to do was ask," he says to her disgustingly.

I cannot help myself this time. "Leave us the fuck alone!"

"Come on, beautiful," says another one. "We just want to hear about your girlfriend's book. Maybe after that, we can watch the two of you do something *else*."

I am horrified, and Charli has tears in her eyes.

"I'm calling the police," she says as she gets out her phone. One of the men, however, reaches for it and loosens her grip, the phone flying onto the ground behind us.

Now, I have been in situations like this before. Not many, but I know what to do.

I laugh. That's right. I laugh.

"Well," I say flirtatiously, "if I had known you boys were serious, I wouldn't have made such a big deal."

They look shocked and confused for a moment. I only wink at them.

"Maybe if you boys buy us some drinks, we'll tell you all about her book," I say with a sweet but playful smile.

When the creeps hit each other on their arms and look at me like I'm a piece of steak, I know I have them where I want them.

"Wow, ok, then," says the one. He looks over at Charli and I give her a quick nod to communicate that I know what I'm doing.

"Damn, you really had us for a while," says another creep with an obnoxious laugh.

"Guys, let me pick up her phone," I start cracking up like this is the funniest thing in the world.

One of the men reaches over to grab it and gives it back to Charli.

Charli, who has thankfully caught on, giggles. "There was no need to scare us like that. Why didn't you just say you boys wanted to get some drinks from the start?"

We have them now. I know we have them now, now that Charli's on board.

"You girls were walking so quickly we thought you were trying to get away from us," says a creep.

"At first, we were. But we never turn down free drinks," Charli laughs. I play along, giving Charli a purposefully sneaky smile as if to say, *Wow! Free drinks! We are so lucky!*

"Well, then, let's celebrate, girls!" says the one with the scar. "We'd be happy to drive you ladies."

Charli laughs. "I don't think so."

"We're not allowed to leave the car here," I explain quickly. "Stupid fucking people, I know. Let's meet you there. Where were you boys thinking?"

They looked a bit hesitant, and I am praying they don't call our bluff.

"McAllister's," says one of them. "You know, right on Route 48?"

"I love it there!" says Charli, being such a good actress that she should really win an Oscar. "What do you say, Kate? Want some free drinks and food?"

"We do get free food, too, right?" I ask them, widening my eyes like a naïve schoolgirl.

The men laugh.

"I'll get you girls," says one of them. "Alright, let's get out of here. You know how to get there?"

"I do," says Charli. "I could really use a cranberry vodka right now."

"Alright, well, cranberry vodka coming up!" says a creep. They begin to walk away.

"See you fine ladies there!" says one as they continue to walk to their cars. "By the way- you're both too good-looking to be dykes."

I shake my head and pull on Charli's hand. We pretend to smile and laugh for a couple of seconds until we get to her car. As soon as we sit down, Charli begins to cry.

"I'm sorry this happened, Kate," she says.

"This is not your fault, Charli. Try to get it together until we're away from them. I bet they're watching us. We have to act like we're going on Route 48."

Charli sniffles but nods and starts the car.

We see the men in their car waiting for us at the end of the parking lot. One of the creeps has his arm out of the window to direct us. We follow behind them for about five minutes before Charli suddenly takes a somewhat risky right turn onto the highway and slams on the gas pedal.

We are now flying down the highway. I look behind me and relax. There is no way those guys can catch up to us now. Not with the traffic and the fact that they did not get on the highway. I breathe a sigh of relief.

Charli still has tears in her eyes. She doesn't say anything until we get home.

"I feel awful, Kate," she says to me as soon as we walk in the door.

"Why do *you* feel awful?" I ask. "It's those fucking morons that should feel awful!"

"I dragged you into all of this," she says, shaking her head. "If you hadn't come with me, this wouldn't have happened to you."

I walk up to her and put my hands on her shoulders. "Thank God I came with you, otherwise who knows what would have happened. I had a great night. You won first place. Don't let a couple of creepy idiots ruin this night for you. They're just jealous that we're sleeping with each other and not with them."

Charli breaks out into a smile. "Well, we definitely showed them who was the boss of us."

I laugh. "We really did. And guess what? We never have to see them again."

She pauses as she puts her purse down on the table. "Did it hurt you, what they said? When they called us that word?"

I shrug. "Not really. I hate that word more than any other word, but who cares? They can go fuck themselves."

Charli breathes a sigh of relief. "Now, we have each other and only each other tonight."

"How would you like to celebrate?"

Charli considers. "Wine on the beach?"

"Perfect idea," I answer. "And Charli?"

"Yes, honey?"

"I really do love you."

She smiles. "And *I* really do love *you*."

Chapter 19

"How's it coming along?" I ask.

Charli and I are sitting at her dining room table, both of us with our laptops open, editing our stories.

"Well, I finally think I know what I'm going to do with my characters," she says with a grin. "You helped me with that."

"How?"

"You said something the other day that really stuck with me," she says, a dreamy look on her face. "You said that one of the biggest tragedies is when two people love each other but cannot be together."

"It's true," I say, stopping to stare into those eyes that hypnotize me every single time.

"I thought a lot about the characters in my story," she continues, "and I think I know what I have to do."

"No," I tell her firmly. "Do not change one single thing about your story. It's perfect."

Charli smiles. "That's what I'm saying. I kept thinking of more for Violet and Melanie to do together. More excitement. But I think the way it is now is the way it's supposed to be. Maybe it doesn't need more 'thrills.' Maybe the thrill itself is in the heartache that comes from not being able to be with someone you love."

At this, Charli puts her hands to her eyes and begins to cry.

I stand up. "Sharon?"

She nods and I hold on to her. I let her cry on my shoulder for a while until she asks that I grab her a tissue.

"I'm sorry," she says. "I don't mean to cry about her."

"No," I say sharply. "I never want you to feel like you can't cry about Sharon in front of me. I always want you to feel like you can talk about her, think about her. I know she is still a huge part of your life, and I know you'll always love her. Charli, that is not a bad thing. I would never want anything different. Do you believe me?"

She looks up at me and nods. Wiping a tear from her eye, she closes her laptop.

"I think I'm finally ready to query," she says.

I smile. "I think so, too. As for me, I need to expand Freya's thoughts more. Make her come alive. Right now, she's a bit silly, don't you think?"

"In the beginning, yes," says Charli honestly. "But with your recent additions and changes to the book, she has become very endearing and honest. Kate, I think you're ready to query, too. It's a beautiful book, honey. It really is. I'm completely in love with it."

I sigh. "I'll believe you. Only because you said so, though!"

Charli sips her tea and looks out of the window. "Kate, look!"

There, flying around, is a hummingbird, darting to and fro like hummingbirds usually do.

"The Universe must agree with us," I say with a laugh.

"I think It does," mused Charli, standing up. "Let's go outside. It's such a beautiful day."

We go outside and sit on Charli's patio, admiring her little garden and the hummingbird that continues to fly around us.

"Can you sing again?" I ask her. "Your voice is so beautiful. You hardly ever sing to me. Sing, Charli."

Charli initially shakes her head, but after some pleading from me, she gives in.

She sings a song that I have never heard in my life, one about honeysuckle and purple violets, and I am entranced. Charli has a voice unlike any person I have ever met. It's pure, clear, soft, and sweet. It is nothing short of enchanting.

Then, she teases me by singing "Billie Jean" enthusiastically.

"You even make a Michael Jackson song sound like a lullaby," I say, reaching out my hand to hold hers.

She laughs and squeezes my hand. "A lullaby?"

"Yes," I answer seriously. "You can make any song sound soothing and pretty. You have the loveliest voice of anyone I know. Did you ever want to be a singer?"

She begins to laugh again, her whole face lighting up and her cheeks turning red. "When I was in high school, my friends and I pretended to start a band for a little while, and I was the lead singer. We didn't get too far. My father was strict and didn't like the idea too much. He'd rather I focus on my homework."

"Oh," I say. "Well, he should have heard you sing. You sing unbelievably. I'm not sure if I could call the sounds hummingbirds make singing exactly, but your voice surpasses them by far. Charli, you could be on Broadway."

Charli shakes her head at me and smiles. "You should hear my drunk karaoke. You might think twice then."

"You're a lot like a hummingbird, now that I think of it," I say, looking over at her. "You're beautiful and elegant, and the most colorful person I have ever known."

"You're sweet."

"I mean it!" I say. "Sing one more song."

And she does, this time a song about an island, and I am captivated again by her voice and am home once more.

"Can you believe we found each other?" I muse. "I mean, of all the billions of people in this world, I got to find you. I am so lucky."

"I'd say I'm the lucky one," she answers, looking into my eyes in that loving way of hers.

"Manny is having another one of his parties," I say to Charli happily one hot August day. "It's this weekend! You're coming with me."

Charli beams. "Of course. I wouldn't miss it!"

I grab her by the waist and kiss her. "You'll get to meet some more of my friends. I'm not really friends with all of them, but there's a couple of people that I am friends with. Rian and Elena are going, too!"

Charli's blue eyes sparkle in that way that they always do. "I'm looking forward to it, Kate."

"Everyone is going to love you," I say enthusiastically. "You already got my closest friends to love you, and that's no easy feat! Especially with Manny. Manny's picky. And Elena can be selfish. Yet, you charmed them all!"

"I'm not sure if I would say 'charmed,'" laughs Charli.

"You are the most charming person I have ever met," I assure her.

"And you, my dear, are the best liar," she teases.

I laugh and give her a kiss on her cheek. I cannot wait until she meets even more of my friends.

Manny's apartment is bustling with people, some of whom I know, and some I don't. As we walk up to everyone, Elena and Rian instantly find and greet us.

"Where's Manny?" I ask, as I don't see him anywhere.

"Where do you think?" laughs Rian. "He's pouring shots over there."

I look towards the little kitchen area and there he is, loud and obnoxious as always, cheering with some friends and drinking up.

"Let's go say hi," I say, pulling Charli with me.

"Hey girlfriend!" Manny yells, giving me a kiss on the cheek. "And you! So glad you came!" he says to Charli, also giving her a kiss on her cheek.

"You have a very cool apartment!" says Charli, looking around.

"Well, it used to be shabby as fuck, but I finally got it decorated the way I wanted it to be," says Manny. "Kate actually painted that one picture on the wall."

Charli looks over at the picture of fire cast in front of a black background, and then at me, surprised.

"Kate," she says in awe, "I didn't know you could paint so well! You've never told me! It's amazing!"

I blush. "It's really not all that great."

"It is, though," she says, walking closer to the picture. "You are even more talented than I knew!"

Manny comes to throw his arm around my shoulder. "You should see her at the bank. She's always doodling something."

I smile and nod.

Charli gives me a look as if to say, *Are you serious?* "Kate. This picture is beautiful. I had no idea you could paint. Why the hell did you keep that from me?"

"Our Kate is very modest," laughs Manny. "But yeah, the girl knows her art."

I smile and shrug innocently.

"I really am beyond impressed," says Charli. "I know you told me you like drawing but this- this is truly remarkable, Kate."

I blush. "I suppose it isn't so bad."

In a moment, another cluster of people swarm the kitchen and Manny is laughing at someone's jokes. Charli and I go to take a seat on the sofa with Elena, who has just gotten here, and with Rian.

"This party is packed!" cries Elena. "Manny is so cool."

"Manny is crazy," teases Rian with a laugh. "But we love him. Hey, Kate, remember at work when Manny got angry and threw the chocolate covered strawberries at Dereck?"

I begin to laugh. I turn to Charli and say, "So one day at work, this guy Dereck-"

"Let me tell it!" interrupts Rian, her hands flying in the air. "This guy Dereck was just a tool. He only worked at the bank for a few weeks and he was the *worst*. Manny hated him, and the two would fight all the time. One day, the two of them got into a fight about something. Do you remember what it was about?"

I shake my head. "Oh, I have no idea. I was only there for the best part."

"Wait, wait, I remember now! Well, Dereck and Manny got into this huge fight and were screaming at each other at work," Rian continues. "and Dereck called Manny a 'fairy,' but in a really rude way. So, Manny gets so angry that he takes a box of chocolate-covered strawberries and starts flinging them at him! One by one!"

I start to collapse in laughter, leaning into Charli. "It was honestly so crazy. I've never seen Manny like that before. What a waste of chocolate-covered strawberries!"

"We have so many crazy memories," continues Rian. "Like the time with that old customer when their dentures fell out in your hand? And when

Robert-" she says, looking at Charli and adding, "he's our boss- asked all of us to clean our desks in silence but then Christina was laughing too hard and then we all got in trouble? Or that time Manny brought Guinness to work and got all of us tipsy?"

We continue to tell funny bank stories until Elena begins to talk about something she saw on TikTok. A few other people have come over now and are talking with us.

"Do you have a TikTok?" Rian asks Charli.

Charli shakes her head.

"We have to make you one," says Elena excitedly. "It's *so* much fun! I mean, everything's on there!"

"Have you guys seen the one with the guy who sings curse words all over New York?" laughs one of Manny's other friends.

"He is so funny!" I agree. "I also can't get enough of that kid who goes around stores and gives the employees funny, fake email addresses."

"That kid is hysterical!" laughs Rian. "Oh my God. Like, I can watch him all day. No cap."

Manny eventually comes around, and soon everyone is laughing, drinking, and playing "Cards Against Humanities" in teams. I am having fun. So much fun, in fact, that I am completely wrapped up in my friends and the game. When I look over and turn to Charli to say something, there is a look on her face that I have never seen before. It is a look of complete discomfort, something that I do not associate with Charli.

"What's wrong?" I whisper.

She shakes her head and smiles, but I know something is up.

"Kate!" shouts my friend Christina, coming over to give me a hug. "Girl, you look great! *Slay!*"

"So do you!" I tell her. "This is Charli."

Christina glows. "Oh, yeah!" she says, looking at Charli. "Kate talks about you at work all the time. Like, *all* the time. She always says how awesome you are. It's so nice to meet you!"

Charli extends her hand and Christina takes it awkwardly.

"It is so nice to meet you, and all of Kate's friends, actually," says Charli with her bright smile. But I can see in her eyes that something is wrong.

"Did you want to leave?" I whisper to her.

Charli waves her hand in front of my face to shut me up, and we all continue playing the game. Charli becomes unusually quiet, so much so that it is very unsettling. It cannot be merely shyness, as Charli was the belle of the ball the last time she met my friends. Perhaps there are too many people here? That must be what is bothering her.

We finish the game and I make sure we stay long enough to have some food. Afterall, Manny will question if we leave too early.

"Now, I want all of us to cheer," says Manny, obviously drunk and holding up his shot glass. "Cheers to friends! Friends forever! I love you all!"

We hold up our bottles and cheer back, the group of us laughing as Manny spills his shot all over the front of his black Gucci T-Shirt.

"You idiot," I tease him. "Stop drinking!"

Manny only laughs. Then he gets out his phone. "Hey, after this, we should all go over to Denver's and have drinks. It's techno night!"

"You don't need more to drink," I chide him playfully.

"But I do wanna dance!" he walks over to me, pulls me from the couch, and starts dancing with me. I pretend to spin and twirl, and the two of us carry on like this for some time until he finally lets go of my hand.

I decide to fake being tired. I don't want my friends to think that Charli is the one making me leave or anything.

"It was so nice to meet you!" gushes our friend Megan to Charli.

"It was very nice meeting all of you," says Charli, waving as we head out of the door.

"Ya'll had better come back here soon," instructs Manny. "Next time, we're doing karaoke!"

"My favorite!" teases Charli.

"Duh," I answer as we shut the door behind us.

When Charli and I step into the car, I touch her hand.

"What's wrong?" I ask her in worry.

She gives me a very sad smile but says, "Nothing, Kate. I think I actually am feeling a bit sick."

"Oh!" I say, turning the car on. "Let's go! We can watch TV and I'll make you soup. How does that sound?"

Charli nods and I drive off. I turn on Spotify and we listen to 80's music, but there is a sick feeling in my stomach.

Charli is not herself the whole rest of the day. I know her well enough to know that something is bothering her, and that she is not actually sick.

"Come on," I say, nudging her. "You can tell me what you're thinking. I know something's wrong, Charli. I'm not stupid."

Charli sighs and looks over at me. I am horrified when I see that she has tears in her eyes.

"Charli!" I cry, reaching out for her hands.

"Kate," she says, now standing up. "We need to talk."

I am too worried and stunned to say anything. I just look at her, my eyes wide and my mouth open.

"This thought has come to my mind before, but I have tried to ignore it," she says, moving away from me and over to sit on a chair.

Again, I say nothing. I am too scared to question her. Instead, I hold my breath.

"Kate," she says, her voice making a choking sound.

"Oh my God," I finally say, leaning onto my knees. "Charli, you're scaring me."

When she looks up at me again, the tears that were making their way into her eyes are now coming down her face. I immediately stand up and run towards her, but she puts her finger out to stop me from bending over to hug her.

"I thought I could ignore it," she says softly. "I really did."

"Ignore what?" now my heart is racing in my chest. "Just tell me, Charli!"

She gives me a look of pure sympathy. "Kate. I know that there is a significant age gap between us. It's never bothered me. But today- seeing you with all of your young friends, in their late 20s and early 30s... I just couldn't help but remember it."

I roll my eyes. "Who cares?"

"I do!" she snaps.

It is so uncommon for her to snap like this that I am stunned.

"This is more serious than we thought," she stands up from her chair and walks into the kitchen. "Would you like some wine?" Typical Charli. Trying to distract from the topic by using wine.

I nod anyway.

She pours herself and me a glass and chugs her own.

"When I was watching everyone laughing and talking, they all just looked so *young*," she continues, her eyes filling up again. "The age gap between us is significant, Kate. You are a mature, grown woman, and it doesn't bother me. But, Kate, I know that someday, this will bother *you*."

I am in so much shock at the words I am hearing that I cannot speak.

"I am fifty-eight-years-old now," she continues. "I'll be sixty-years-old in a couple of years. You're not even thirty-five yet. You have your whole life ahead of you." Here, she pauses to take another sip of her wine. "I cannot hold you back anymore."

I am breathless. I can only stare at her for a full minute before saying, "What?"

"You have your whole life ahead of you," repeats Charli, wiping her wet cheek. "You have so much time to meet other people, fall in love, get married, even have children…"

"No," I say, beginning to take in what she's saying more fully. "I want to marry *you*. I want to be with *you*. I don't give a shit how old you are."

"Listen to me," she says so sharply that it shuts me right up. "You're thirty-three. You have so much life ahead of you that you haven't lived yet. I will only be holding you back. As I get older, you'll still be young for a very long time."

I cannot believe what I am hearing. "You have to be joking. Charli, I don't care how old or young you are. I love you. I thought you loved me, too?"

Charli's voice sounds strained as she chokes, "I love you more than words can explain. I love you more than anyone in the world. I love you more than I have ever loved anyone before."

"Ok then! That settles it." I take another sip of wine and lean against the counter, trying to look casual. "Hey, maybe we can go out for dinner tonight? I still wanted to take you to that vegan restaurant I was talking about."

Charli looks up at me and I know it then. I can just see it in her eyes. I know we are not going out to a restaurant tonight. I also know that we most likely will never be going to a restaurant together again. Once Charli sets her mind on something, that is what it is going to be. There is no changing it.

"I can't do this, Kate," she says, now letting the tears come. "I've thought about it more and more, and I've tried to shrug it off, but I've been so selfish." She comes over and puts her hands to my face. "I love you so much."

"No," I say, taking a step back. "Don't do this, Charli, don't do this."

"I have to," she says in barely a whisper. "Do you want to take care of me in thirty years when I'm too old to walk and you have to change my diaper in a nursing home?"

I force myself to laugh. "Sure. I don't care. Charli, I'm not a baby. I'm thirty-three. I'm a grown woman. I can make my own choices."

"I know you can," she says. Then she pauses before saying, "I can too."

I sigh, the tears now coming down my own face. "Don't do this, Charli. Please. I don't care about your age. I never did. Not once! I don't care. I love you! Don't do this.

Now the two of us are holding hands as I beg and plead for her to stay.

"I cannot be selfish any longer," she says, this time firmly. "I have to let you go. It's the hardest thing I've ever had to do, but I have to do it. I cannot hold you back any longer. You will find someone else, someone closer to your age, someone who can be there for you for the rest of your life."

"No!" I cry in a panic. "Charli, no! Stop all of this. I don't care! I love *you*. I love *you*! I don't care about anyone else! Please, Charli. I don't care. I love you so much. You're the only one I want to be with."

Suddenly, Charli walks away and goes upstairs. I follow her, yelling at her to come back down, but she doesn't listen to me. Instead, she starts throwing her things into her bag.

"Put it down," I beg her. "Put down the goddamn bag!"

She gives me a look full of remorse, those eyes of her burning right into my soul, and walks out of the room. I follow her down the stairs, crying for her to stay.

"Please don't go," I beg. "Let's talk about this. You went to a stupid party with my friends. That's all."

"Honey, it's not just the party," she says. I can hear it in her voice. There is a finality in it that I have never heard before. My heart breaks into pieces. "I've had these feelings for some time, but I've tried to push them aside. I have to do what is best for you, not what I want. I can't give you everything you need. I refuse to hurt you."

"If that's true, then you won't do this," I can barely utter the words.

"I love you so much, my Kate." Standing by the front door, she puts her hand to my face. "It's better this way, I promise you. I'll always be here if you need me, but we need space. I can hardly bear to do this, and it's taking all of my energy, and I need time."

"Fine," I say, crossing my arms. "Take some time. Take today and tomorrow. In a couple of days, you will come to your senses."

"No," she says, this time so harshly that I take a step back. "I have to let you go."

With that, she opens the door and walks out. I follow her, shouting for her to come back, but she gives me a sad look and steps into her car.

"I'll call you tomorrow," she says. "I love you."

I'm crying too hard now to say it back. I watch her drive away, a sick feeling in the pit of my stomach.

When I turn around and walk back into the house, there is an emptiness inside that I have never felt before. Not even after Richie left. There is also a hollow space inside of me where my heart once was before it dissolved into tiny fragments in my chest.

"No!" I sob into my hands, my body leaning against the kitchen wall as I sink down onto the ground.

Lila comes over and starts licking my hands. I cannot believe what is happening. I take my phone and throw it across the room. Lucky for me, the phone lands on the living room carpet.

I have to let you go. Those terrible words ring over and over again in my mind.

I stand up and run to the phone, hastily calling Charli. I leave three voicemails before texting her to come back. Hours pass and I am just sitting there watching the phone in total silence, poor Lila now sleeping next to me on the couch. I don't even listen to music. I am too distraught and too much in my head.

Charli doesn't answer me at all that night. Instead, I sit alone, begging the Universe not to take her away from me again.

Chapter 20

I end up falling asleep on the couch. When I wake up the next morning, Charli still has not called or texted me back. I call Elena and tell her what is going on before I take a walk. I want to get away from my own head, which I obviously cannot do, but at least I can pretend.

When I come back inside, Charli has continued to ignore me. I try to distract myself by going onto the computer, then on TikTok, but everything reminds me of Charli.

It is not until 1pm in the afternoon when Charli calls me.

"Oh my God, I was so worried!" I cry into the phone, already starting to sob. "Are you ok?"

"Physically, yes," she says. "Kate, you have some of your things here. I will gather them up for you and you can come by to pick them up whenever you're ready. Just tell me when you're coming over. I may not be home when you're here, but just come in and grab everything."

I clutch my chest, feeling actual physical pain. "You cannot be serious. We aren't breaking up."

"Kate," she says harshly, "I love you, but this is for the best. I need to give you space to process your grief. I need to process mine, too, and we can't do it together."

"Charli, please-"

"Text me when you're coming," she says shortly before she hangs up.

Of course, I get ready to go to her house. I will certainly *not* text her that I am coming, otherwise I know she will leave her house. No. I am going to make her talk to me.

As I practically stomp out of the house, keys dangling from my hand, I pause in my tracks.

How could she do this to me?

Suddenly, I am struck with a dreadful thought. She never loved me. This is just an excuse, her way of getting out of the relationship. If she really loved me, she would be fighting for me.

I hold onto my chest again as I digest this thought. I turn around, unlock my door, and go solemnly back inside, Lila rubbing against my ankles. I plop my purse on the ground, not caring where it lands, and go to sit on the couch. I have stopped crying now but my eyes are so swollen from the day before that they ache.

I look into my phone, see the background picture of me and Charli laughing that time we went to the aquarium, and then stare at the wall for about an hour.

"This is an excuse," I say out loud to Lila. "She doesn't love me. She just wanted an escape, so she's using our ages. She knew how old I was from the start, and it never bothered her before. Suddenly, it's a big deal? No. This is what she wanted all along."

I think over our brief but powerful relationship. I go over and over in my head the things I may have said or done wrong. How could the Universe give me my soulmate only to take her away from me so soon?

Anger is now mixed with my grief. In fact, I am so hurt, so angry, that I go into my bedroom and scream into my pillow until my throat is sore. I cannot believe this is happening.

Charli calls me a couple of hours later. I don't pick up. Now, *she* can be the one to panic.

I know being angry is better than being sad, so I turn on angry break-up music and sit on the couch with a cup of coffee. Of course, my love for Charli trumps any little bit of anger I am experiencing, but I must at least keep *some* of the anger. If not, I will completely crumble.

Charli tries to call me two more times. I ignore them. Then, I get a text from her.

"Kate, please call me back."

I toss my phone to the side and cross my arms. This time, *she* can be the one to know what it feels like to be sick with dread, wondering what is going to happen next. *She* can be the one to hurt.

"I'm not fucking answering," I say to Lila, who looks at me like I have lost my mind.

Charli continues to try to call me, but I refuse to answer. I am so hurt by her actions, and so very pissed off.

"I'm coming to your house if you don't pick up," she texts me.

Suddenly, the pain and anger that has been meshing together all comes out. I pick up the phone and call her back.

"Kate, you had me so worried!" she cries into the phone.

"Well, now you know what it's like," I hiss, pursing my lips.

"Kate," she says, her voice cracking.

"Don't," I say, this time sharply. "You never cared about the age difference before. Now, it's suddenly a problem for you? How stupid do you think I am? I'm not buying it. You just wanted an out from our relationship. You *wanted* to leave! You could not care less about me."

"That is not true!"

"I'll pick up my things tomorrow after work," I say curtly. "I'll come by around six. That way, you'll have plenty of time to leave the house so you don't have to see me. In fact, I prefer that you do."

"Kate," she repeats, and I can tell she is crying. "I really do love you!"

"Don't," I tell her. "If you really loved me, you'd be here fighting for me. And you know it!" I press the "end call" sign and begin to sob into my hands.

I stand up and throw the now-empty wine bottle at the wall. It cracks, fragments falling to the floor, just like I do.

The next day I call out of work. I am too heartbroken to do much of anything, and Manny will know something is wrong. I don't want to explain this to my friends for as long as possible.

I get out my phone and text Charli, "Just keep my things. I'm not coming over. It's only some clothes and my toiletries. I have more. Just keep them."

I bite my lip to keep from crying. If I cry anymore, my eyes might fall out of their sockets.

"Are you sure, Kate? I can bring them to you."

"I'm sure," I answer back.

Well, Charli finally has what she wants. She is no longer tied up with me. She's free to move forward with her life, while I will forever be heart-broken.

I am so angry that I am seething. How could she do this to me? How could she, after knowing everything I have been through? After everything we've been through together? After knowing how much I adore her and need her?

I hate her, I say in frustration.

Of course, it's not true. But I love her so much that I pretend to hate her. Otherwise, I am not sure if I am going to live through this.

I dramatically fall to the floor and bury my head in my hands. The memories I have of the two of us convolute together, all of the good times and the bad. I have never felt an ache like this before. Sure, I have been hurt. But this isn't simply being hurt. This feeling inside of me is burning my chest and sinking into my stomach. There is a hollowness where my heart once was and the world around me is unclear and blurry, and not just from the tears.

What will I do now?

I wrap blankets up around me, Lila now purring at my feet. Somehow, even though I continue to cry, I eventually fall asleep.

A week goes by. A dreadful week where I have done nothing but look at our pictures and sob. My friends have begged to see me but I have refused them all. I do not want to be interrupted from my overwhelming grief.

Charli tries to text and call me, but on Tuesday I ask her to stop. I tell her that I will not be able to move forward if she keeps talking to me. She respects my wishes and does stop contacting me. The silence hurts terribly, but it is what I need.

It's now Friday night. I have been able to use my vacation days to take off work. I just cannot bear for Manny to pry into my life and make me talk about this. I just cannot do it yet.

Charli's voice wrings through my head. *I have to let you go.*

It makes me angry every time I think of it- every time I remember that she just let me go without a fight.

Against my better judgement, I decide to go online and look at Charli's writing page. I haven't so much as glanced at anything online of Charli's, but my curiosity gets the better of me.

Her most recent post has a picture of a hummingbird on it. The caption reads, "Recently, I have gone through some of the worst struggles of my days. I have lost someone so important to me, and I love this person with all of my heart and soul. She thinks that I wanted to get away from her, but this couldn't be further from the truth. Sometimes, we must let people go. Not because we don't care or love them, but because we know that they are better off that way. Sometimes, we have to sacrifice a little bit of our own happiness so that a person we care about doesn't end up getting hurt.

"It's true that the Universe leads us to different people. And it is also true that we can have soul connections with many different people. Loss is not easy. Many years ago, I lost someone very special to me. She had cancer and passed away very young. Watching her die was the hardest thing I had to do in my life. It broke me to pieces. Watching someone you love so much, someone who had so much life, wane away like that is unbearable. As much as it hurts to let someone go, sometimes we have to, so that we are not selfish and can let them move forward. Sometimes, even when people care about each other, it's better to let go for the other person. So, I think I understand the lesson now. Sometimes love is letting go."

I am speechless. I burst into tears and clutch my chest. All of the fury that has been stewing inside of me floats out of my body like a ghost and now all I can feel is the grief. I think of her story of Violet and Melanie. I remember the amazing person Melanie was created from, Sharon, and how much Charli went through when she passed away from cancer. I know this affected Charli deeply and will continue to affect her the rest of her life. Perhaps she doesn't want to put me through this same grief someday.

Charli has a point. As much as I don't want to believe her, she has a point.

I want nothing more than to be with her forever. However, my version of forever and her version are different. As much as I love Charli, I realize with a sick feeling that this entire time, she was actually trying to do what was best for me, not hurt me. Instead of continuing a relationship with me, she decided to sacrifice her own happiness so that I could avert more heartbreak later on.

If it was up to me, I would never let her go. I can't say I agree with her decision. I don't agree with it, in fact, although I do understand it now. I would do anything to be with Charli for all of my days. In her eyes, although the age gap itself is not a problem, I know now that Charli was worried that I wouldn't have her for as long as I would need her. She knows that someday, she will most likely go before me, and then I'll have to spend many lonely years without her.

I begin to cry. I take out my phone and call her.

"Kate," she says softly. "I'm glad you called."

"I understand," I say through my tears. "I get it now. I understand the lesson."

"Oh, Kate," she says, her voice still soft. "You know I'll always love you, right? And I'll always be here if you need me?"

I wipe my nose. "I'll always need you, Charli. That won't change. But I understand better than I did before. You don't want me to go through the pain of your loss someday."

"Yes," she answers. "I can't bear to think of it, Kate. I love you so much!" here she stops, and I can tell she is crying. "I love you enough to set you free."

"I won't be free," I sob. "I'll be trapped in the cage of my grief, forever wanting you."

"You will move on with time," she says.

"No," I say determinedly. "I won't ever move on. Not from you. You mean everything to me and so much more."

"But you understand where I'm coming from?"

I can hardly speak now. Instead, I hyperventilate into the phone, "Yes."

"I will be here for you always, as a friend," she says sternly. "Ok?"

I bite my lip, trying to gain some composure. "Me, too," I barely manage.

The two of us continue to cry on the phone for a minute. I know this is already so hard for her. And I realize that I love her enough to make this easier for her.

"I'm going to hang up now," I say, forcing myself to stop crying. "I'll always be in love with you, Charli."

By the way she is sobbing into the phone, I can tell that this is hurting her just as much as it's hurting me. "I love you, Kate," she manages before I end the call.

When I turn around, I am forced to face my own emptiness. I scream and sob into my hands. Nothing has ever hurt me like this before. It's because I have never really been in love before since finding Charli.

I know I will never be the same. Charli came into my world and touched it like the sunlight hitting the Earth. She forced me to look at who I really was, the woman I was becoming. She made me realize that I had been pretending to be someone for so long, just trying to fit into a world that never understood my heart. She opened my eyes and taught me what it was like to love- not just to feel love, but to fight for love, too. To give up everything for love, to sacrifice for love, to embrace love- and also, to love someone enough to let them go.

Although this pain feels unbearable right now, I know that Charli's love has given me a strength that I never knew I had. As I slowly walk over to sit on the couch, I happen to catch something flying right by my eye. There, outside of the window, is a little hummingbird, flying to and fro, as if trying to come inside. It moves its elegant and agile body around, and I am mesmerized by its natural beauty. I can't help but smile to myself.

When the bird finally flies away, I am tempted to drink, but I am so sad that I cannot even do that. Instead, I slowly stand up and make my way upstairs to my bedroom. There, I stay in bed the rest of the day and night. I don't eat, and I only get up to use the bathroom. My heart is shattered to pieces, and it hurts to even breathe.

Against my better judgement, I play *Love Song* by Lana Del Rey. It is our song, the song she subtly dedicated to me in her post last year. It breaks my heart even more to listen to it now, but I don't want to move on. I never want to move on from Charli. I love her so much and I never want to forget any of the moments we shared, no matter how brief our relationship was.

The next day, instead of sitting on the couch and feeling like death itself, I go upstairs into my little office and open up my laptop.

I take a deep breath, click on Word, and type at the top of the first page:

THE LULLABY- by Kate McMullin.

I now know that it's true. Charli came into my life for a reason, right when my soul needed her the most. And now, instead of writing some silly, whiny, predictable book, I feel that I have the courage to write something truly remarkable, something real.

I think back to all of those years ago when I met her. I think back to when I found her sitting alone at the dining hall and I went to go speak to her. She looked gorgeous that day.

I remember her kindness when she offered to review my story. I remember the beautiful book she wrote and the sorrow it brought to my heart. I remember how hurt I was at her feedback on my story and all of the horrible, angry, terrible things I said to her. I remember begging for her forgiveness and sending her the hummingbird figurine. I remember trying uselessly to manifest her back into my life, some way, somehow. I remember getting up the courage to send her that one last message and my joy when she actually responded.

I think back to that first time I saw her after nearly thirteen years. She just brought her energy and her light right inside the café with her. I think back to the first time we kissed that night on her couch, the first time we made love, the first time she told me she loved me.

She was the calm in my storm, the heat to my coldness. How would I be able to live without her fire?

Some people are together for fifty years and do not love each other. Some people are together for only a few months and love each other with all of their hearts and souls. Soulmates are soulmates, and it doesn't matter the conditions. It doesn't matter the age gap, the background, the circumstances, or even the time known.

Love shows up in many forms, in many different ways. Love is not always easy, and it can hurt a lot, and it isn't always pretty, but it is always real. Love is the most authentic feeling in the world, because it cannot be helped. It may be slightly tamed, or stuffed down, or ignored, but it is always there no matter where it is lurking in the corners of our hearts and souls. Love is both inspiring and dangerous, because it makes us question everything we once knew. It makes us see things in ways which we never have before and do things we would never usually do. It can make us crazy, it can make us blind, it can make us change our minds about everything we used to hold true.

My love for Charli will never die. There will never be a moment when I will not love her. And, although I feel completely incapacitated by grief, at least her love will never leave me. I will always have it. And, in that way, we will always have each other.

Chapter 21

Later in the week, I sit on the beach in silence, pondering what I have learned over the year. I truly feel as if I have grown up and matured in ways that I didn't even know I needed to. This time last year, I was avoiding my own emotions, pretending to go along with what everyone else thought I should be doing. I was married to the wrong person, hiding my own identity, and grappling with my sexuality. Now, I am confident as a lesbian and even proud of myself for the journey it took to get me here.

I let the wind make my hair stick up on all ends as I think back to times Charli and I have sat on this very beach. This time, though, I am all alone. This time, I have no hand to hold, no bright eyes to look into, no one to dance in the waves with me. This time, I don't have the love of my life by my side.

I am reminded of Violet and Melanie's love story, and the way Charli wrote so beautifully what it is like to truly love someone so much that it gives your life meaning. I am also reminded of the time we ourselves slept on the beach, letting the salt and sand invade our noses like a gentle perfume and the sound of the water expressing its passion onto the shore. The memories I have here are truly and inexplicably sacred. And although Charli is thankfully very much alive, the absence of her presence still causes me much grief.

I faintly wish to see a hummingbird. I know that I won't, as that would be too wild of a coincidence, so instead I open up my laptop and continue writing my story. I am still torn between making a happy ending or a sad ending. Should the characters be blessed with the love that I was forced to walk away from? Or should they experience the heartache and pain, just like I do?

As much as it pains me to do it, I choose the sad ending. I want the love story to be a perfect fairytale ending, but that wouldn't really be real life, right? At least not without some major bumps in the road. I have learned that true love is not just being with a person but having the courage to sacrifice one's own happiness for the betterment of someone else.

As the waves crash in front of me and the sea gulls squawk around me, I find myself smiling unexpectedly. Charli would say that everything happened as it was meant to be, that the Universe conspired for things to be just as they are now. She would see the positives in this break-up, and she would teach me how to move forward in a way that is kind, loving, and purposeful.

I sigh and get out my phone. It's been a few weeks now, and I want Charli to know that I still do not hate her, and I understand why she had to do what she did.

"I'm at the shore writing a book," I text her. "I'm thinking about you. That's all I want to say. I just wanted you to know that."

In less than a minute, she responds. "I was just thinking about you, too. Well, I always am. I always will."

I smile again and tuck my phone into my pocket. I then begin writing the first sentence of the book I will write. This time, I decide to tell the story- the story of me and Charli. It is a bit scary to put everything out there like that, but it is the brave and right thing to do. Some stories need to be told, and this is one of them.

I sigh as I type, thinking of exactly what I want to say. Then, it comes to me.

I write, "I nervously wring my hands as I stand in the auditorium…"

TWO YEARS LATER

"I am *so* proud of you!" gushes Elena as I sign my fortieth copy of my new book, *The Lullaby*.

After a couple of hours, the big crowd is finally

starting to die down a bit and I can finally breathe.

It's taken me a couple of years, but my book has finally been edited exactly the way I want it to be. Thanks to my amazing literary agent and publishing team, I am beyond thrilled to see my book finally in print. Now, with the help of my friends, including Richie- who has just left to get to work- I am once again a celebrated author.

"Thanks for helping," I say to Elena. "I wouldn't be able to do all of this without you."

"Gee, thanks!" says Olivia, hitting my arm. "What about your perfect girlfriend? Huh? What about *me*?"

I laugh and playfully hit her back. "That goes without saying, babe."

Olivia gazes into my eyes, looking at me like I am the greatest thing the earth has ever seen. For a moment, I am totally captivated.

"Get a room," Elena laughs as I hear a couple of people walk over.

I smile. I am feeling so happy and fulfilled in this moment. I finally got my book published, a book that actually means something to me, and it's already sold thousands of copies.

"Oh my God!" cries Elena in shock.

I turn around to see what she's looking at and my mouth drops. There, standing with an older man, is Charli.

When she looks at me, I feel all the old emotions come back. This time, however, I feel them in a different way- more like a memory.

"Kate," she says, her whole face glowing. She is wearing a cream-colored coat and toffee-colored boots and gloves. She is as stunning as she's always been.

My eyes fill with tears. "Charli." I cannot help but leave my table to run and hug her. "Charli! I haven't seen you in years! You look beautiful!"

Charli's eyes fill up as well and she holds me close.

I turn around and point behind me. "That's Elena, remember? And that's my girlfriend, Olivia."

Charli raises her eyebrow in interest and walks closer to the table. I notice now that she is holding on to the man's hand. I momentarily feel stung, as I had not expected this. However, it is not in the same way as before.

"This is Charli?" asks Olivia in shock.

I nod and smile. "The famous Charli Diaz herself!"

Charli laughs and picks up a copy of my book. "As soon as I heard on Facebook that you would be here, I knew I had to come. I can't wait to read it, Kate."

"You might find some parts familiar to you," I tell her.

She smiles. "What a beautiful title. I can't wait to see what it's about."

"Well, I wrote it about an old friend of mine," I say mysteriously. "She was a good friend who changed my life and made me see the world in a different way. She also taught me that sometimes love is letting go."

I can tell that Charli is trying not to cry. We both reach out to hug each other at the same time and let the tears come.

"I'm sorry," she says. "I didn't mean to come here and ruin this big night for you."

"You haven't ruined anything," I tell her. "I'm glad you came."

Charli turns to Olivia. "You are so beautiful!"

Olivia blushes. "I've heard so many good things about you." Olivia knows every single thing about me, including what I went through with Charli, and has never once judged us for our choices.

"It's such a pleasure to meet you," Charli answers. "This here is my fiancé, Rob."

Rob, who looks about Charli's age, gives us a smile and shakes our hands. I think, for his age, that he is quite handsome. There is a small part of me that feels a little prick of pain when she says the word "fiancé," but I do not feel upset about it or sad. I am actually very happy to hear that Charli has found someone to love.

After all the introductions, Charli insists I sign her copy of my book. In a minute, a new crowd of people swarm up to get copies. I see Charli, who is watching me on the side with a very proud look on her face.

"What's your book about?" asks a man at the table.

I look over at Charli and smile. "Hummingbirds."

He gives me a curious look. "*Hummingbirds?*"

"The book is about love and the lengths we go to find it," I say more seriously. "Hummingbirds are just a part of it. What the story is really about is having the courage to love someone else, and to do what is right for the person you love, no matter what that may be."

"I see," says the man with a shrug. "Sounds like it'll be right up my wife's ally. I'll get one. Hey, can you sign it?"

"Sure," I say, taking my pen in my hand.

When he walks away, I turn to my friends. "Thank you for coming here."

I notice Charli has walked away from the table with the book. I come over to her and I see that she has her hand to her face and is wiping away tears.

"Charli!" I cry, "Are you ok?"

"Kate, I'm more than ok," she answers.

Then, unable to speak, she points to the first page of the book and the dedication. For there, in big letters, it says, "Dedicated to an old friend- one who taught me what it means to love. Sometimes, we have to let go of someone we love. Instead of keeping them locked up in a cage, sometimes we have to let the hummingbird free."

About the Author

Kirsten Miles is a mental health therapist in the heart of New Jersey. She works with clients who present with anxiety, depression, and various other diagnoses. She has published a couple of poems, including "If Love was a Color" in the 2019 edition of "New Jersey's Best Emerging Poets 2019: An Anthology." She has also self-published an award-winning novel titled "Senior Year" under the pseudonym of Lily Caverton, which details mental health issues. She currently lives with her amazing wife, Clarissa, and their two dogs, Jack-Jack and Ruffles, whom she has many adventures with!

You can learn more about Kirsten by visiting her website at KirstenMiles.com.

Made in the USA
Middletown, DE
15 August 2024